Parting words . . .

"You've made my life here bearable. I don't know what I would have done without you. But . . ."

"But you don't belong in Bitter," she said, her voice wistful.

"Look Ellie," he said anxiously. "We'll see each other again. Just as soon as I've made some money . . . as soon as I'm somebody. And . . . and in the meantime, we can write."

"Yes, we'll write," she whispered. Although the pain was killing her, she knew she had to let him go now, but her fingers were numb from holding on so tightly. She let them slide to her side and took a step back.

For a long time he stared at her in silence as though he were memorizing her features, then he turned away.

"Goodbye, Ellie," he said softly.

"See you, Jesse," she whispered to the empty darkness.

Dear Reader:

Romance offers us all so much. It makes us "walk on sunshine." It gives us hope. It takes us out of our own lives, encouraging us to reach out to others. Janet Dailey is fond of saying that romance is a state of mind, that it could happen anywhere. Yet nowhere does romance seem to be as good as when it happens *here*.

Starting in February 1986, Silhouette Special Edition is featuring the AMERICAN TRIBUTE—a tribute to America, where romance has never been so wonderful. For six consecutive months, one out of every six Special Editions will be an episode in the AMERICAN TRIBUTE, a portrait of the lives of six women, all from Oklahoma. Look for the first book, *Love's Haunting Refrain* by Ada Steward, as well as stories by other favorites—Jeanne Stephens, Gena Dalton, Elaine Camp and Renee Roszel. You'll know the AMERICAN TRIBUTE by its patriotic stripe under the Silhouette Special Edition border.

AMERICAN TRIBUTE—six women, six stories, starting in February.

AMERICAN TRIBUTE—one of the reasons Silhouette Special Edition is just that—Special.

The Editors at Silhouette Books

BILLIE GREEN
Jesse's Girl

Silhouette Special Edition

Published by Silhouette Books New York

America's Publisher of Contemporary Romance

SILHOUETTE BOOKS
300 E. 42nd St., New York, N.Y. 10017

Copyright © 1986 by Billie Green

ISBN: 0-373-09297-0

First Silhouette Books printing March 1986

America's Publisher of Contemporary Romance

Printed in the U.S.A.

BILLIE GREEN's

college professor once told her that she was a *natural* writer. But her readers and editors find it hard to believe that she writes one good story after another only because she comes by them naturally. Maybe someday this devoted wife, mother of three and romance writer extraordinaire will create a heroine who is a writer. Then, possibly, we will get a hint of her trials and tribulations.

TEXAS

Underlined places are fictitious.

Chapter One

June, 1974

Ellie slowed her confident stride to lift her head and inhale the smell of the field around her. The hot air seared her nostrils and the smell of dried broomweed stung the back of her throat.

In the distance she could see Bitter, Texas, her hometown. Waves of heat rose from the cement streets and brick buildings. Bitter in June was pretty much like Bitter at any other time of the year, except maybe hotter.

While the country in general was held in thrall by the ominous spell of Watergate, and Texas in particular was wondering if the current drought would equal the devastation of the fifties, in Bitter the main topics for the month of June were the reopening of the Majestic theater, the fact that the mayor's wife was once again redecorating their ranch-style home, and—in whispers—the rumor that Mrs. Thalia Sharpe had begun an affair with Harvey Ledbetter from the tool and die factory.

In a barren-looking field on this particular day in June, Ellie made her way quickly through the hardy growth. Her pink, sleeveless blouse and carrot-red hair made a splash of unexpected color in the midst of the tan and brown landscape. As surefooted as a mountain goat, she walked barefoot through the field, sidestepping thorny branches, stinging nettles and red antbeds.

This was Ellie's world and, as she passed familiar landmarks—the remains of a brick well and the brushpile that had served as den to many generations of jack rabbits—she seemed very much a part of it. However, her eyes reflected the fact that her thoughts were far from Bitter and the surrounding terrain.

Even if Ellie had read Dickens, she wouldn't have called it the worst of times. At seventeen she wasn't the least bit interested in politics; the summer heat didn't bother her; and if she had known about Mrs. Thalia Sharpe she would have laughed. She might very well have called it the best of times because in June of 1974, Ella Mae Cooper was in love.

As she cut across Mr. Purley's field, she laughed simply from the joy of being alive. Bitter was not a perfect place to live even in milder weather, but it was all Ellie knew and sometimes when overcome by her ebullient emotions, she even thought it was beautiful.

The end of Mr. Purley's field brought her to the vacant lot behind the variety store. Bending down, she slapped at the pale brown dust that clung to the tops of her feet before slipping them into the worn sneakers she carried slung across her slender shoulders.

The main part of Bitter, the business section, consisted of four short streets enclosing a town square. The larger businesses—the lumberyard, the tool and die factory and the gravel pits—were all outside the town. The town proper contained small adjoining buildings that housed such necessary emporiums as the hardware store, the five and dime and the Curl Up and Dye Beauty Salon. Each storefront held a sameness, resembling one another as they all resembled the pale brown dirt that surrounded the town.

Behind the single row of buildings, Texas took over in the form of prickly pear cactus, short, thorny mesquite trees with heat-yellowed leaves and acres of water-starved weeds defiantly growing in the bare dirt and rock. Johnson grass and tumbleweeds grew right up to the back doors of the town.

Once on the street Ellie glanced around, her eyes expecting and finding nothing new to record. As her gaze caught a display, she slowed, then stopped in front of Dowe's Variety Store, wondering ritually why they called it a five and dime when there was nothing in the store that could be had for a nickel.

For a moment she considered breaking into her small savings to buy a tube of black mascara, then she sighed and shrugged. Even if she bought it, Grannie Jean most likely wouldn't let her wear it.

Jesus died for our sins, Ella Mae. You can't pay Him back by acting bad. It would hurt Him.

It looks to me like He would be too busy watching out for the Russians to worry about me wearing eye shadow, Grannie.

Ella Mae Cooper, you don't make fun of the good Lord. Do you hear me?

Yes, ma'am. I'm sorry.

Giving a rueful laugh, she shook her head, her short red hair swirling untidily around her face. No, Grannie Jean definitely wouldn't let her get away with mascara.

If she could just make the trip into Odessa, Ellie could go to one of the discount stores and get a white midriff-hugging blouse like the one Kathleen Dowe had worn the night before at the skating rink. But Odessa was one hundred and fifty miles away and even if Grampa was up to the trip, their old Ford wasn't. It hadn't been out of the garage since the previous January when Grannie had sprained her ankle and had been unable to walk the six blocks to church.

Although it was convenient, sometimes it annoyed Ellie that everything in Bitter was within walking distance. As a child she had found the sameness of the small town of eighteen hundred comforting, but now the idea that the town was just plain boring was beginning to dawn on her. Bitter didn't carry the luxuries that made life interesting, only the necessities for people who were just able to make ends meet.

Sometimes when Ellie would lie in the stiff grass watching the high, small clouds drifting slowly over her world, feeling their shadows touch her face and move on, she would wonder what life was like beyond the city limits of Bitter. What would it be like to be a seventeen-year-old girl, right on the brink of womanhood, in a town that had traffic lights and people on the sidewalks that you hadn't known all your life?

She smiled slightly as she turned away from the window and fixed her eyes on the Pixie Drive-in at the end of the street, then she began to walk again. Most of the time Ellie was too busy to wonder what else was in the world. After all, Jesse was in Bitter. What else did she need?

"Ella Mae Cooper!"

Recognizing the voice, Ellie caught her breath and quickened her steps. Maybe she could ignore him. Maybe he would think she hadn't heard him call her. Jesse would have thrown back a wisecrack and kept on going.

"Ella Mae! Come here, girl!"

Turning in resignation, she walked slowly in the opposite direction. Ellie wasn't as brave as Jesse. No one was as brave as Jesse.

Squinting against the sun, she could see Chief of Police Sharpe standing in the doorway of the Eat Shop, the inevitable toothpick stuck between his teeth. Her heart began to beat a little faster as she walked. The head of their small police force was a large man, and his brown uniform was stretched tightly across his stomach. The sunglasses that were almost a part of his face never failed to set Ellie's nerves on edge. They were a smooth, black expanse of glass that seemed to see everything and approve of nothing.

She tried now to imagine him as he looked in church, for on Sunday mornings Chief Sharpe became an ordinary, overweight man in a ten-year-old blue suit who allowed his children to quarrel through Pastor Hall's sermons.

She failed to conjure up the comforting figure and all she saw was the brown uniform and the hard, frowning face. Her heart was pounding painfully as she stopped in front of him. If there was one thing Grannie had taught her, it was a healthy respect for authority.

"You seen Jesse, honey?" he asked, his square red face changing expression as he gave her an indulgent smile.

"Is something wrong, Chief Sharpe?"

"Someone broke into high school last night, Ella Mae, and tore up a bunch of band instruments." He threw down the toothpick in disgust. "I've already tried talking to that worthless daddy of his, but you can't get a word out of the drunken fool."

It was obvious Chief Sharpe was annoyed. When he breathed hard the button that rested on his middle quivered and, for the first time since he had hailed her, Ellie felt like laughing.

"Mr. Catlin donated those instruments," he continued. "And he's good and mad." He caught and held her eyes. "I want to talk to Jesse about it."

She swallowed with difficulty. Mr. Catlin owned the gravel pits where Jesse worked, and the feed store, and the hardware store, and anything else in Carrol County that Mr. Dowe didn't own. Mr. Catlin could do just about anything he wanted. Hadn't he caused the Gonzaleses to pack up and leave town simply because they were Mexican? What chance did Jesse have against that kind of power?

In a hoarse whisper she said, "It couldn't have been Jesse. Jesse was with Sidney last night."

He snorted. "You know that don't mean a thing." Under his breath he muttered, "Damn lazy coloreds," then shook his head and gave her a sympathetic look. "Sidney was probably right there helping Jesse tear up those instruments, Ella Mae. You know they're as thick as thieves."

"But..." She inhaled to keep from shaking. "But Sidney works hard, Chief Sharpe. He's not—"

His icy stare cut off anything else she had intended to say. After a moment, he smiled. His teeth were discolored and wide-spaced, always seeming too big for his mouth.

"Your Grannie Jean done a real fine job of raisin' you, Ella Mae," he said. The knowledge that his words praised her docility made her redden with shame, but she held her silence.

"You tell Jesse when you see him that I'm looking for him. And when I get through talking to him Mr. Catlin has a few things he wants to say. I believe between the two of us we'll find out what happened." He turned away, then glanced back, his face set in determined lines. "And if I don't find him, I can always haul him off his job come Monday."

He walked back into the café, releasing her. As she flew down the street toward the Pixie, she mentally whipped herself for not standing up to him. Jesse would have. Jesse wouldn't have let him call Sidney a lazy colored. It was only because she was a girl that Chief Sharpe called him colored. To a man he would have talked differently.

Ellie had heard on television that things were changing for blacks in the United States. Someone must have forgotten to tell the citizens of Bitter about it. Here things moved at a slower pace, and change came so slowly it was barely noticeable.

The current hairstyles and fads in clothing never made it as far as Bitter. They were foibles of the outside world. And any kind of interference from the outside world was not appreciated, even in the form of help. During the drought of the fifties the area could easily have been declared a disaster area, but the ranchers didn't go to the government; they went to Mr. Catlin and Mr. Dowe for loans to restock their devastated ranches. They knew the interest would be high, but they also knew who ran the county.

Ellie let out a sigh of relief as she walked into the air-conditioned dining room of the Pixie. She stood quietly at the counter waiting for the young woman in blue denim to notice her. At the back of the grill area, she could see Sidney, but his head was lowered as he worked.

"Whatcha' need, Ellie?"

"Just ice water, please."

The woman frowned as though giving Ellie a five cent cup of water would cause a cut in her paycheck, then turned to scoop ice into an orange paper cup, fill it with water and hand it to Ellie with another frown.

After giving Sidney another hopeful look, Ellie walked over to a booth and sat down, a frown dimming the natural glow on her small face. She had to find Jesse and let him know that Chief Sharpe was looking for him. Sidney would surely know where he was.

Glancing up, she saw Sidney nod to Mrs. Higgins, the manager, as the large woman gave him an abrupt order, then he turned to put another load of plastic dishes in the huge silver machine. When he finished, he looked up and Ellie motioned frantically. Giving a short nod of his head, he turned to speak in a low voice to his boss, always keeping his eyes on the ceiling or the windows, anywhere but on the woman who barely acknowledged his request as she threw two more buns on the grill.

"Hey, Ellie. What's up?" he asked cheerfully, his casual manner totally at odds with his earlier demeanor as he joined her at the booth. He wiped long brown fingers on the apron that enveloped his tall frame then sat across from her. "You look like you did when Grannie Jean found out you'd been smokin'."

"Chief Sharpe is looking for Jesse," she said in a breathless whisper.

He spat out a casual vulgarity. "What does that bastard want now? Jesse's going to get sick of the way Sharpe rides him one of these days. And when he does—" he shook his head "—I don't want to be around."

Ellie didn't want to think about what would happen to Jesse if he tried to fight Chief Sharpe. She stared at the ice melting in her cup, then said, "He said Jesse broke into the high school last night and tore up some band instruments."

"That's a lie and Sharpe knows it." Sidney's thin face registered his anger. "Jesse was with me last night."

"I told him that, but he said you were probably in on it with him." She paused, her face reddening with emotion. "Chief Sharpe is such a . . . a turkey."

Sidney leaned back in the seat and laughed. "Grannie Jean sure put a lock on your tongue, didn't she?"

Ellie grinned. "Don't ever tell her, but I swear in my head. It just won't ever come out of my mouth." She glanced down at the ice again. "I hope I didn't get you in trouble, too, Sid."

"Would you stop worrying?" He reached out to give her hand a squeeze in exasperation. "You worry all the time over Jesse. You can't start worrying about me, too. Maybe one of these days you'll figure out that your worrying doesn't do any good and stop it. You know how mad it makes Jesse."

"I don't think I can stop now, Sid," she said, her lips curving in a wistful smile. "It's a habit." She leaned closer. "Do you know where he is? I need to let him know Chief Sharpe is looking for him."

"Yeah, he said for you to meet him at the cabin."

Three minutes later Ellie was making her way toward the alley that ran beside the fabric shop. If she cut through the grounds of the Golden Years nursing home she would be at the bottom of the hill at the back of Otis Bates's property. And on top of that hill, Jesse waited.

"Ella Mae."

Stepping into the alley, Ellie looked over her shoulder when she heard her name, then winced. It was Mrs. Russell, the organist for the Friendship Baptist Church.

"Hello, Mrs. Russell," she said. Ellie didn't stop but merely walked backward as she talked, inching her way into the alley. Mrs. Russell could talk a rattlesnake into submission and Ellie knew the woman would hold her up for thirty minutes if she let her.

"Ella Mae, is your grandmother coming to choir practice this Wednesday?"

"I don't think she said, Mrs. Russell." She was almost free. Two more feet and she would be out of the alley. When the pavement ended and West Texas took over, Ellie turned and ran, calling back over her shoulder, "I'll tell Grannie to phone you. Goodbye, Mrs. Russell."

"Ellie, wait!"

Ellie pretended not to hear and disappeared into the brush, knowing she would soon be out of range.

The cabin Ellie was headed for was actually an old wooden storeroom that Mr. Bates hadn't used in

years. It had been Ellie and Jesse's secret meeting
place for as long as Ellie could remember and as she
ran through the dense thicket of post oak and cedar
that overran the property she whispered a prayer that
Jesse would still be there, hoping God would over-
look the fact that she had been rude to His own organist.

It was cooler under the trees, but the air was heav-
ier. She shoved cedar branches out of the way as she
ran, and her skin itched where they brushed against
her. She had to be more careful here than she had
been on flat ground because of the solid rock pushing its way up through the prickly grass.

When she reached the base of the hill she stared
ahead for a moment as though she could see through
the dust-colored trees and dust-colored rocks. She
felt sorry for farmers like Otis Bates. It was hard
country to farm. The cactus and mesquite had taken
over most of it, and the only people who made it here
were rich enough to have extensive irrigation sys-
tems. Nothing grew tall in this country; everything
was short and twisted, but there was strange beauty
in the barrenness. And there was a different kind of
beauty in the tenacity of plants and people who lived
here. They hung on even when it was smarter to let
go.

Chief Sharpe hung on, too. He hung on to Jesse
like a leech. Why was he like that? she wondered as
she ran with increased urgency. What had started the
whole thing? She knew Jesse's pickup was too loud
and sometimes too fast. And maybe he did get into
too many fights. But the trouble he was involved in

was always harmless and couldn't explain the way the police always questioned him about everything from obscene phone calls to robbery.

With her mind working double time, Ellie tripped over a rotting log and almost lost her balance, causing a small brown lizard and several frantic bugs to scurry away in protest as she disturbed their home under a pile of leaves. Glancing up, she saw an outcropping of rock. She was almost there.

A tree supported his back as Jesse rested his tanned forearms on his knees and stared at the cigarette he held between forefinger and thumb, watching the thin stream of blue smoke.

Leaning his head against the hot bark, he frowned, wondering if Ellie would be able to make it today. Mrs. Cooper could take it into her head to clean the whole house and Ellie would be tied up for hours just when Jesse needed her, just when he was bursting to share this with her.

For as long as Jesse could remember he had been sharing with Ellie, sharing his small triumphs, his devastating defeats. She was the only one who would understand. He didn't think it at all strange that he, a grown man of twenty-two, should have such a close relationship with a kid like Ellie. In fact, he never stopped to think about their relationship at all. It simply was.

Leaning forward, he stubbed the cigarette out in the dirt, his strongly molded lips twisting in a smile. For nine years he had watched out for Ellie, advised and scolded her, and he was careful not to examine what he felt for her in the light of day. For although it made him extremely uncomfortable, he knew at the heart of his friendship with her was a feeling of ownership. She belonged to him, to do with as he pleased.

And today he needed her to share the greatest triumph of his life. He needed to tell her about Kathleen.

When Ellie finally saw the clearing ahead, she was out of breath. She paused on the edge, her eyes quickly searching the area. Then she saw him and her heart flip-flopped the way it always did when she came upon him unexpectedly.

He sat just outside the shack with his back against an ancient mesquite tree. Worn, tight Levi's molded thighs that five years in the gravel pits had made hard and muscular. A black T-shirt lay like a dull glaze on his chest and upper arms. His dark hair was too long, an unruly lock falling across his brow. His face and arms were dark, too; years under the relentless sun had seen to that. But the sun hadn't tampered with the sensuous lips that could smile so beautifully but were all too ready to sneer. He looked like a rebel. He looked ready for a fight as though it would only be a physical extension of the battle going on within.

Ellie's careful examination had taken only seconds, but it was all the time that was needed for the wealth of feeling that had been growing inside her to explode like a Fourth of July fireworks display. She had never imagined that love would be so overwhelming, overwhelmingly beautiful and overwhelmingly painful. She loved Jesse Perkins with an obsessive depth that frightened her at times.

Drawing in a breath to steady herself, she stepped into the clearing. "Jesse." The word was an urgent whisper as she ran to him and dropped to her knees beside him to grab his arm. "Jesse, Chief Sharpe is looking for you again. He said—"

He grinned as he took in the dirty streaks on her face. "Hold on a minute, Peanut. Don't get so excited. Sit down and catch your breath before you try to talk."

"But, Jesse—"

"Sit down." He pulled at her waist until she sat down beside him.

When her breathing slowed, he said calmly, "Now you can tell me what all the excitement's about."

"Someone broke into the school last night and messed around with the band stuff." She couldn't be as calm as he and the words tumbled out hurriedly. "Chief Sharpe and Mr. Catlin think it was you."

He shrugged. "So what else is new?"

Raising up on her knees so she was again eye level, she stared at him anxiously. "But he's looking for you. He wants to question you about it."

"I'm sure he'll find me...when I let him. Tom Sharpe couldn't find his ass if he had a road map leading him right to it," he said with lazy contempt.

He didn't sound at all worried and Ellie felt like moaning in frustration. Sometimes she just wanted to grab Jesse and shake him until his teeth rattled.

She sat down again, resignedly crossing her legs in front of her yoga-style. After a moment she said quietly, "Jesse, why does the chief hate you? Did you do something to him?"

He shook his head. "Not that I know of. He hates me because I'm poor."

"I'm poor and he doesn't treat me like he does you. Anytime anything happens he's on your doorstep to question you. Even when he knows good and well it wasn't you. I just don't understand."

He smiled then, but it wasn't a pleasant smile. "Tom Sharpe treats Sidney like he's simpleminded because he's black. He treats you like you're a cute pet monkey with no feelings or brains because you're poor. But you see, you're poor and respectable. Sidney's black and respectable." He bent his head back, staring at a hawk circling overhead. "He hates me because I'm white trash. His job lets him say yes sir and no sir to people like the Catlins and the Dowes. An added bonus is getting to push around people like you and Sidney. That makes him somebody in Bitter." He shrugged. "But it wasn't all that long ago that Tom Sharpe was white trash, too. Looking at me makes him remember that and he doesn't like to remember."

Her gray eyes flashed angrily. "But you're not white trash," she protested. "That's a stupid thing to say. You work hard and you're a good person. Besides, you're the smartest person I know."

"And just how many people do you know?" he asked, laughing as he gave her short hair an affectionate tug, then he took an unfiltered cigarette from a battered pack and lit it. "No," he continued, shaking his head, "my old man's a drunk and my mother was a whore. That makes me white trash."

She caught her breath and felt all her muscles tense. Jesse never talked about his mother and Ellie was glad because now his mouth twisted with angry cynicism, making him look a decade older than his twenty-two years.

When she started to argue, he cut her off and for the first time she noticed a gleam of excitement in his dark eyes. "How come you're not mad? You always get mad when he starts picking on you." At this, his smile grew bigger. "What's up? You look like you just won a million dollars."

He shook his head. "This is better." He paused. "You know the dance tonight at the VFW lodge?" When she nodded, he said with exaggerated nonchalance, "I may be going to it."

She stared in open-mouthed surprise. "You're not! You never go to dances. You said they were silly."

"They are silly, but it doesn't matter. I'll go anyway because . . ." He stopped to inhale slowly, then said, "Kathleen may be going with me."

Ellie held herself still as a white-hot pain pierced her chest. And just for a moment she felt disoriented as though a hole in the earth had opened up and she had fallen through. She swallowed hard. "You asked Kathleen to go to the dance with you?"

He nodded, excitement and pleasure shining from his strong features. "And I think she's going to say yes. You know what that means? If she goes with me everyone will know that she's my girl. We won't have to meet on back roads anymore.''

Ellie was the only one who knew he had been seeing Kathleen secretly. At least twice a week Jesse and the girl Ellie had sarcastically dubbed the Prom Queen would meet and drive in Jesse's pickup to a deserted road somewhere. Ellie didn't want to think about what they did then.

In fact she didn't want to think about Kathleen at all. The Prom Queen was a coward, but Ellie couldn't tell Jesse that. Kathleen didn't deserve to be Jesse's girl. He should have someone who would be proud to be seen with him. Someone like Ellie.

She could feel Jesse watching her as she drew abstract figures in the dirt with her finger. "If Kathleen won't go," she said suddenly, "will you take me?" At his soft chuckle she glanced up to give him a pleading look. "Please, Jesse. I've never been to a dance before.''

He laughed harder and even though he was laughing at her, Ellie loved the sound. "You're just a kid," he teased. "Kids aren't supposed to go to dances. They're supposed to play with dolls.''

"I'm not a kid. I'm only two years younger than Kathleen." She inhaled and glanced pointedly at her high, rounded breasts. "I'm growing up. Honest, Jesse.''

He spent a moment looking at her breasts, too, then grinned. "They're coming along real nice, but who in hell told you they're more important than your brain?''

"You did," she muttered stubbornly, then allowed a small smile to appear. "At least that's what you said about Patsy Summers."

"That's Patsy Summers. Not you. You've got a real brain, a damn fine one if you'll ever remember to use it."

She sighed, knowing the subject of the dance was closed. "Why do you talk like that, Jesse? Like someone from up north."

"Because it annoys the people in this town when I talk better than they do." He shifted his weight slightly and picked up a rock, hurling it far into the trees. "Don't you ever wonder why people talk about 'up north' like it's a whole different country? 'Oh they're from up north.' Like they're from Russia or something. The people around here think the Far East begins somewhere around St. Louis. Doesn't it ever make you wonder?"

"No, it doesn't," she said emphatically. "I wonder why God gave me freckles even on my stomach, but 'up north' is too far away for me to worry about."

He grinned at her then wiped the sweat from his face with the bottom of his shirt. "Speaking of your freckles, Peanut, don't you think it's time you cooled them off."

Ellie was more than willing to get rid of the dust that covered her and before he had finished speaking she was on her feet, racing toward the creek that ran behind the shack. In most places the creek was shallow and would dry up later in the summer, but behind their secret place was a wide, deep swimming hole fed constantly by an icy spring.

Ellie unbuttoned her cotton blouse as she ran and when she reached the steep bank, she stripped it off, kicked off her shoes and began to unzip her faded jeans.

Jesse hadn't moved as quickly as she and, pulling the jeans down her legs, she watched while he peeled the black shirt over his head. His skin glistened with sweat, the muscles in his back tautening as he leaned over to remove his Levi's. His body was tanned all over, even beneath the white, cotton-knit brief, she knew, and the muscles rippled slightly in the sun. He reminded her of a wild horse she had seen once. He was strong and lean, the lines of his body clean and hard. He was all muscle and fiery pride.

She shook her head suddenly and looked away as he turned toward her. Grannie Jean would have a fit if she knew Ellie had looked at a man's body in that way, but just for a moment she wished they still swam in the nude as they had when she was a child. Something was happening inside her body and it made her want to see him, to touch him and have him touch her.

She heard the splash as his body hit the water, then he shouted, "Are you going to come in or are you going to stand there all day?"

"Hold your horses," she said, and stuck out her tongue. She frowned as she glanced down at the plain cotton bra and panties she wore. Grannie Jean didn't buy anything that wouldn't hold up for years. She knew it really didn't matter. Jesse had seen them a hundred times before, but just this once she wished they were lacy and feminine instead of practical and durable.

Shrugging, she grinned at Jesse and jumped in beside him, dousing his face with water.

Jesse watched as Ellie surfaced several feet away from him. "You better stick close to me, Shrimp. A granddaddy catfish could just swallow you whole."

"It didn't hurt Jonah much," she laughed, arching her back to dive deep. When she came to the top, she tread water and said breathlessly, "Norma told me how to get taller. She said if I stood on my head for two hours a day it would stimulate my pituitary gland."

He snorted. "Norma hasn't got the brains God gave a pissant, you idiot. If you stand on your head for two hours a day all you'll get is a flat head and floppy ears."

Laughing, he dodged the wave of water she pushed at him in retaliation. With her hair slicked back, the delicate line of Ellie's cheekbones became visible, and for a moment he simply stared at her. What had happened to the baby fat that surely was there yesterday?

She looked like a mermaid as she lay back and floated lazily on the water. What was she thinking? How long had it been since Ellie told him about how she felt and what she dreamed?

Swimming over to her, he brushed a strand of hair from her eyes. "You know, Peanut," he said in wonder, "someday you're going to be a beautiful woman."

Ellie shivered suddenly. Jesse's words didn't please her; they hurt. She knew that someday was no good. She wanted to be beautiful now because now was when Jesse was ready to fall in love. She swam away from him and waded out of the pool, shaking the water from her hair with awkward movements.

"I have to go, Jesse." She didn't realize how sharp her voice sounded as she began to pull on her clothes. "Grannie Jean will start worrying."

He gazed at her for a moment in surprise. He had never heard Ellie so abrupt. She was growing up, he thought sadly, feeling almost bereft as he followed her out of the water. He sat on a stump, studying her thoughtfully while she dressed.

What was this sadness that was suddenly attacking him? Things were just beginning to go right for him—weren't they? Although logically he knew that time had to bring change, Jesse stopped thinking for a moment about what he would gain. As he stood to put on his clothes, he wondered for the first time just exactly what he would lose.

Chapter Two

The house Ellie had called home since her parents' death on her eighth birthday was small and plain. There were a hundred just like it in Bitter, but Grannie Jean had made this one unique by giving loving care, and lots of water, to the small patch of ground that surrounded the white frame structure.

Pansies and zinnias and four o'clocks covered every inch that wasn't claimed by the green carpet of grass. Rose moss filled an old washtub beside the porch; petunias spilled over a border provided by a discarded tire. Morning glory vines shaded one end of the high, wide porch while honeysuckle overran the other.

All the luxurious growth would not have been possible had the Coopers not been fortunate enough to have their own well. It meant Grannie Jean could water her small garden to her heart's content. It also meant a lot of hard work because with sufficient water there were enough tomatoes, cucumbers and black-eyed peas in the summer to be canned for the winter.

The house next door to Ellie's provided a startling contrast to her own neat yard. Here weeds grew knee high and there wasn't even a chinaberry tree to break the penetrating rays of the West Texas sun. The screen door hung drunkenly on one hinge, and the windows were covered by time-yellowed sheets.

Jesse and Ellie avoided looking at the house next door. It was Jesse's home, and it provided nothing but pain and embarrassment for either of them.

As they stepped into the small living room a multitude of smells greeted them—fresh-baked chocolate cake, lavender bath powder, pine-scented cleaner and the Johnson's paste wax that Grannie Jean used to put a high gloss on the room's hardwood floor.

It was the smell of the chocolate cake that lured them into the kitchen where Ellie's grandmother was putting the last bit of white icing on the newly baked cake.

"I figured the smell of this would reach you two wherever you were." Grannie's words always sounded like a scold, even her caring words. But words didn't count with Grannie Jean. Everyone knew what was in her heart.

Ellie's paternal grandmother wasn't a large woman, but she was comfortingly round. There was only the tiniest bit of gray streaking the long brown hair that she wore twisted in a bun at the base of her neck.

"Well, don't just stand there," she said to the meek faces still hovering in the doorway. "I suppose you think you both deserve a piece. Since coveting is a sin I'd better feed you to keep you out of hellfire."

"Oh, we know we don't deserve it, Mrs. Cooper," Jesse said, his smile widening, his eyes sparkling in a way that would charm a bobcat out of a tree. "But just the smell of your cake is worth a small trip to hell."

"You're a heathen, Jesse Perkins," the older woman said as she lay a slice of cake on a saucer. Although her voice was properly condemning, there was an answering smile in her eyes. "And don't try to deny it. I've always said you were a bad influence on Ella Mae."

Ellie laughed as she pulled a two-gallon glass jar of raw milk from the refrigerator. "I can stand a brush with this particular heathen, Grannie, but I'm beginning to wonder about you."

"You flirting with my bride again, Jesse?"

They all turned as Ellie's grandfather walked into the room. Ralph Cooper was a small, lean man, standing no more than five feet tall. His sallow face was dotted with brown age spots, and a pink scalp showed through his thin white hair. A stroke three years earlier had affected the left side of his body, leaving him with a slow, lopsided gait. The stroke hadn't touched his sense of humor though, and the milkiness that the years had brought to his blue eyes hadn't subdued the constant twinkle.

"I'm trying, Mr. Cooper," Jesse said solemnly. "But I think she prefers older men."

"I prefer men who have a lick of sense," Mrs. Cooper said sharply. "It's a real shame there don't happen to be any like that in this room."

"Why Jeanie," Mr. Cooper said in surprise. "You didn't say nothing about sense when you were snuggling your cold feet up close to mine last night."

"Ralph!" she gasped, then turned to the two sitting at the table. "Stop that giggling. I thought I taught you two to be respectful of your elders."

"You did, Grannie," Ellie said, grinning widely. "But you forgot about what Grampa was teaching us behind your back."

Her husband was laughing harder than Ellie and Jesse when Grannie Jean ordered him to sit down and stop cackling. As she cut another slice of cake she said, "How's your daddy, Jesse? I took him some of my homemade soup this morning and it seemed like he was feeling better."

The whole town knew Daryl Perkins was an alcoholic, but Grannie Jean refused to acknowledge the fact. She always said Jesse's father was "feeling poorly" and no one had enough nerve to contradict her.

"That was real nice of you, Mrs. Cooper. I'm sure the soup is just what he needs." Jesse's words were polite, but Ellie could see the cynical look in his eyes and it hurt her.

Swallowing the last of his milk, he turned to Ellie. "I guess I'd better be going, now. I have to talk to . . . someone."

Kathleen, Ellie thought. That's who he had to talk to. He had to ask Kathleen again if she would go to the dance with him. Ellie felt the smile on her face become plastic as she walked with him through the house and onto the porch. She leaned against a square column as he headed for the gate in the white picket fence.

"Jesse," she said hesitantly, biting her lip when he glanced over his shoulder. "What if Mr. Dowe gives you trouble? You know he doesn't like you."

He shrugged. "I'm not worried about Mr. Dowe. Kathleen's the only one I care about."

She felt a knife-sharp pain in the region of her heart but didn't let it show on her face. "He's her daddy. He can stop you from seeing her if he wants to."

"Don't look for trouble, Peanut," he said softly. "It'll always find you without any problem at all."

Before she could argue the point, they heard a voice from the house next door.

"Jesse."

Ellie saw Jesse's face freeze, and she turned slowly to see his father standing in the doorway of Jesse's home. Daryl Perkins wasn't an old man by any means, but years being best friends with a whiskey bottle had added a slack grayness to his square face. His clothes were wrinkled, his straight brown hair tangled and falling forward across his forehead.

"Jesse, I can't find my dictionary. I've look..." The slurred words trailed away when he saw Ellie on the porch. "Afternoon, Ella Mae. You—you look real nice in that pink blouse."

"Thank you, Mr. Perkins. How you feeling to-day?"

"Better, honey. I'm feelin' a lot better. I had a pain in my leg last night, but—"

"Daddy," Jesse interrupted, his eyes closed tightly for a moment in embarrassment. "Your dictionary is on the chair beside your bed where it always is. I saw it there this morning." He paused and when he opened his eyes, just for an instant Ellie could see raw pain. "Don't you think you should lay down a while? You don't want to tire yourself out just when you're feeling better."

Tears formed in the older man's eyes. "You're a good boy, Jesse." He shifted his gaze to Ellie. "Isn't he a good boy, Ella Mae?"

She nodded, feeling all her muscles stiffen along with Jesse's. "Yes, sir. He's a good man," she amended quietly.

"Go lay down now, Daddy," Jesse said, his voice gentling as though against his will.

"Yes, I guess I will. The dictionary must be under my shirt. I shoulda'..."

His voice trailed away and Jesse didn't look back to see the loving concern that was etched in Ellie's face.

"I'll see you, Ellie."

"See you, Jesse," she whispered hoarsely.

At seven that evening the summer sun was still streaming brightly into the living room. Ellie sat in a worn wingback chair, one leg swung over the arm as she thumbed through a magazine. She felt restless, itchy, and couldn't think of anything but Jesse. Grampa sat on the couch in front of the wide window that overlooked the street. When he let out a low whistle, she glanced up.

"My goodness, somebody sure looks nice this evening," he said mysteriously.

"Who?" Then she remembered Jesse's date and repeated, "Who, Grampa?"

"Who? Who?" he echoed. "Your feet don't fit no limbs. Why don't you come and see?"

She knelt on the couch in time to see Jesse pass the house. His hair, neat and slicked back, was still damp from a shower. He wore a soft gray shirt, brand-new Levi's and his polished boots almost outshone the large Western belt buckle at his waist.

Kathleen had said yes. Ellie had tried not to believe that the pampered Prom Queen would finally get up enough nerve to defy her father and the town, but obviously she had.

Sliding back off the couch, she walked slowly to regain her former position on the chair, but the pages of the magazine were a blur before her disturbed gray eyes. She glanced up at last to find Grampa staring at her with sympathy marring the twinkle in his eyes.

Standing abruptly, she said, "I think I'll see if I can help Grannie in the kitchen."

"You do that, sweetheart," he said gently as she left the room.

Grannie Jean was putting up a small batch of pickles, and after fifteen minutes she turned to Ellie in exasperation. "Ella Mae Cooper, that's the third time you've washed those cucumbers. I appreciate the thought, but pickles without rinds will be a little limp."

"I'm sorry, Grannie." She paused, staring out the window at the mimosa that stood in the center of the small backyard, then said hesitantly, "If you don't mind, I think I'll walk up to the Pixie."

Grannie Jean stared at her for a long moment. "No, I don't mind," she said finally. "But you be sure and start home early so you won't be on the street after dark."

"Can I wait for Sid to get off work and ride home with him?"

"I guess so. You're too fidgety to stay around here." She paused. "Is something bothering you, honey?"

Ellie shook her head. She didn't like lying, but she knew Grannie Jean's sympathy would break her. "I guess I've just got growing pains."

The heat of the day had mellowed a little as she walked the six blocks to the diner. The sun was going down and on the horizon charcoal-drawn trees stood bold against a peach-colored sky. This was the peaceful time of day when it seemed that even the dogs were too awed by the beauty, or relieved by the diminishing heat, to bark.

When she walked into the drive-in, the small dining room was almost empty. The two Purley children were noisily sharing a banana split and Faye Little, one of Bitter's three beauticians, sat at a booth drinking a Coke while she waited for her husband to close the Fina station and pick her up.

Ellie read all the titles on the jukebox even though she knew she wouldn't waste a dime by playing a song. When Sid called to her, she looked up and waved then went back to reading the song titles.

The words all merged in her mind, becoming tangled with the confusion of her emotions. Things were beginning to change. She felt it in the pit of her stomach and it scared her. What was she going to do without Jesse?

She moved in a daze to a booth at the back of the room. Now that everyone knew he and Kathleen were an item, Jesse would be spending most of his time with the Prom Queen. And what would happen if they got married? Mr. Dowe would most likely make him a foreman or even a supervisor at the tool and die factory, and then Jesse wouldn't ever want to see anyone from their side of town. He would be mixing with the numerous Dowes and Catlins who owned everything worth owning. Mr. Dowe even owned the Pixie Drive-in where she sat at that moment.

She felt a painful lump in her throat. Jesse had said that Chief Sharpe didn't want to remember what he used to be. Would Jesse be the same way? Would he try to forget Ellie?

For hours, Ellie sat alone with her thoughts. When darkness fell completely, she didn't even notice the change. By the time she finally glanced around her, the room was full of people and the noisy clatter of forks against plastic dishes.

Suddenly Sidney was in front of her, offering her a malt-filled paper cup before flopping onto the bench seat across from her. "You sure are thinking hard. Don't you have anything better to do on a Saturday night?"

"Thanks, Sid," she murmured as she took a sip of the chocolate malt. "What would you suggest? Grannie didn't want me to help her with the pickles and Grampa always watches Saturday Night Wrestling."

"Where's Jesse?"

She glanced up and her features froze. After a moment, she nodded toward the door. "There."

Sid turned sideways in the booth then whistled long and low under his breath as Jesse and Kathleen walked into the Pixie. "So she finally got up enough stomach to meet him in public."

"Did you know about Kathleen?" she asked in surprise.

"I guessed. There were too many nights that Jesse was busy. And any fool could see the way he always looks at her." He turned back to Ellie. "Don't let it bother you too much, Ellie."

"Is that something else any fool could see?"

"If you mean does everyone know you're in love with Jesse, then no," he assured her. "I can see it because the three of us are always together. As far as everyone else is concerned we're all just good friends."

"I think Grampa knows. But it doesn't make any difference as long as Jesse doesn't." She grinned crookedly. "Can you imagine what he would say? He would yell a lot about how stupid I am, but he would really feel like he had let me down by not loving me back."

"Jesse loves you, Ellie."

"I know; just like you do." She swallowed the lump in her throat. "But it's not the same."

Suddenly Jesse and Kathleen were standing beside them. "Hi, Ella Mae. Hi, Sidney," Kathleen said. Her personality could only be described as bubbly. "What are ya'll discussing so seriously? Did the Russians attack while we were at the dance or something?"

Ellie wondered if she was biased or if Kathleen was really as dumb as she sounded. "Hi, Kathleen, Jesse," she responded quietly. "Did you have a good time at the dance?"

Kathleen was quick to answer. "It was fabulous. Mrs. Simpson fixed the cutest crepe paper honeysuckle vines all over the walls of the lodge and the band came all the way from Odessa."

As she described the fruit punch in detail, Ellie glanced surreptitiously at Jesse to share her amusement with him. But Jesse wasn't amused. He was staring at Kathleen as though she were an ancient sage and her every word golden.

Examining his face, Ellie was attacked by a strange, sad feeling. Jesse couldn't even see that the girl beside him was silly and artificial. It wasn't jealousy Ellie was feeling now. It almost seemed like mourning for a lost friend.

She glanced up when Sidney slid out of the booth. In his eyes was an echo of her own concern.

"My break's over," he said grimly. "I guess I'd better get back to work. You want a lift home, Ellie?"

She nodded and smiled. "It's the only way Grannie Jean would let me stay out after dark."

As he moved away, Kathleen leaned closer, avoiding contact with Sidney, and said, "Your Grannie Jean is just the sweetest thing, Ella Mae. You see this dress here. Well, when Mama and I got it home from Dallas—where we had bought it at Neiman's—we found out it was just the tiniest bit too big in the waist." She smoothed her hand over her midriff, inhaling so her full breasts were even more prominent. "Mrs. Cooper said sure she could fix it for me, and it didn't even take her two days to finish it so I could have it to wear to the dance tonight. You be sure and tell her I said I was tickled with the way it looks. And any time I need alterations done, I'll surely bring them to her."

"I'll tell her," Ellie said, smiling until it hurt. "I'm sure she appreciates your business."

"We'd better go sit down, Kathleen." Jesse glanced down at Ellie. "I'll see you tomorrow, Ellie."

Kathleen laughed gaily as they walked away, shaking her blond hair back over her shoulder. Ellie stared after them, wishing she could do something very unladylike to that perfect hair and perfect figure.

"It won't take her long to get tired of him."

Ellie swung around. In the booth behind her was Palmer Catlin, as blond and attractive as Kathleen.

Like Ellie, Palmer was an orphan, but that was where the resemblance ended. Palmer was the ward of John Catlin and that was all that ever needed to be said.

"Your eyes are turning green, Palmer," she said calmly, squelching her own jealousy. "You're just mad because you know Jesse's better looking and smarter than you are."

"I'm not mad," he denied with a shrug. "Let Kathleen have her little fling. Her father and my uncle won't let it go on too long." He smiled. "They decided a long time ago that Kathleen would marry me."

What Palmer said could very well be true. The Dowes and the Catlins had been business partners and friends for generations. A marriage between Palmer and Kathleen would be welcomed.

"They may just decide to break it up tonight," Palmer continued, "if Uncle John finds out it was Jesse who wrecked the band equipment."

Ellie refused to let him see that the threat bothered her. "You know good and well Jesse didn't have anything to do with that."

He rested his chin on the arm he had slung over the back of the booth. "I don't know anything of the kind and neither do you." He smiled. "And even if he can't prove it, Uncle John may not want Jesse Perkins working for him when he finds out he's messing around with Kathleen."

"Your uncle is a big bag o' wind, just like you are, Palmer." Ellie's voice was stiff with anger. "Why don't you go pester someone else?"

Realizing he had finally penetrated her armor, Palmer gave a satisfied laugh and stood up to walk toward the table where Jesse and Kathleen were seated.

"You sure are a scrappy little devil, Peanut."

She swung around. Luke Owens was standing behind her leaning against the booth.

"What is this?" she asked, raising her eyes to the ceiling in exasperation. "Do I have a sign on my back that says Please, Somebody Bug Me." She frowned up at the stocky young man. "I thought I told you not to call me Peanut."

"Because your precious Jesse calls you that?" He glanced toward the front of the room. "It looks like Jesse has something else to keep him busy tonight."

"He's not too busy to take care of you, Luke." She nodded toward the grill. "Neither is Sidney. Is there something in particular you wanted or did you just suddenly feel like being obnoxious?"

As fire leaped in his hazel eyes, Ellie wondered if she had gone too far this time. She didn't like being intentionally rude, but Luke had been trying to get at her since school let out. It was as though he had decided she was finally grown up and therefore fair game. Ellie had come to view him with contempt because he never spoke to her in front of Jesse or Sid. He knew they would both fight him if they found out he was bothering her.

Moving closer, he ran a finger slowly over her hand as it lay on the back of the seat, sending shivers up her arm. "I just wanted to see if maybe you had changed your mind about going out with me now that Jesse has Kathleen."

She pulled her hand away and hid it in her lap. "What Jesse does has nothing to do with me. I've told you a hundred times—I don't like you."

The fire she had seen before was nothing to what blazed in his angry eyes now. "What in hell makes you so high and mighty?" he spat out in a vicious whisper. "You live on the same side of town I do. What makes you better than me?"

"I didn't say I was better than you." She kept her voice firm. She couldn't let him know he made her nervous. "I just said I didn't like you. I don't like the way you bully people who are smaller than you and I don't like the way you drink all the time."

His short laugh was filled with contempt. "You don't act so particular around old man Perkins—and he's the biggest drunk in town."

She swung her head around sharply to make sure Jesse hadn't heard, then turned back to Luke. "You just better not let Jesse hear you talking about his daddy like that, Luke Owens." She clenched her fists in her lap. "Please go away or I'll call Sid."

His eyes narrowed, flashing venom. "Just wait, Ellie," he said, his voice taut and low. "Jesse and Sid won't always be around. Then we'll see who bosses who around." His steps were awkward when he moved away as though he held his whole body in tight control.

Ellie had heard Luke's threats before. They didn't frighten her. She simply wanted him to stop bothering her. Putting him out of her mind, she watched

Jesse and Kathleen from the corners of her eyes,
their heads close together as they stared across the
table at each other in a way that sickened her. In de-
feat she dropped her eyes to the melted malt on the
table.

Jesse couldn't believe how beautiful Kathleen was.
He couldn't seem to take his eyes off her. Everything about her was perfect, her smooth, creamy skin
showing not one blemish. He could almost understand the thinly veiled anger with which her father
had greeted him earlier. When Jesse had arrived at
the Dowe house to pick Kathleen up for the dance,
Mr. Dowe had hovered over them like an avenging
angel, fury and contempt written on his face.

Exhaling slowly, Jesse charted the loveliness of the
face across the table. If he could own something as
perfect as Kathleen, he knew he would guard it just
as vigilantly.

But Jesse was determined to show Mr. Dowe, show
the whole town of Bitter, that he was somebody. No
one would try to talk down to him when Kathleen
Dowe walked beside him.

Glancing up, he saw Palmer watching them closely
and smiled inwardly. Palmer didn't want to admit
Jesse had beaten him. He had tried to make trouble
several times during the dance. He had tried his
damnedest to make Jesse feel awkward and out of
place. But it hadn't worked. It hadn't worked because Jesse was Kathleen Dowe's date.

Suddenly he caught a glimpse of Luke Owens and
frowned. He didn't like the way Luke watched Ellie

all the time, the way he ran his eyes over her body as though she were for sale. Jesse felt a sharp, inexplicable tightening in his stomach. Ellie wasn't a child anymore. The way Luke looked at her made that obvious. She definitely didn't need to have someone like Luke Owens hanging around her, he thought grimly and decided then that he would have a little talk with Luke real soon and make sure he understood that he had better leave her alone.

"Jesse."

Kathleen's voice, as smooth as honey, pulled his eyes back to her.

"Daddy told me I have to be home early tonight." She reached across the table to touch his face with one slim finger. "I'm sorry we won't have time to go to our spot, but—" the look she gave him as she paused caused his heart to start pounding in his chest in anticipation "—maybe tomorrow night."

A nod was all he could manage as he stood and pulled back her chair. Before they could move away from the table Palmer stepped in front of them, blocking their way. "Does your daddy know you're out with garbage, Kathleen?"

Ellie's head jerked up at Palmer's words. She could see Luke and a group of his friends standing to one side grinning broadly. She knew they would get a kick out of seeing Jesse humiliated.

"Have you got something to say to me, Catlin?" Jesse said quietly.

Palmer gave him a look of mock-surprise. "I believe I was talking to Kathleen."

"Look, man," Jesse said wearily, "you caused enough trouble at the dance. I don't think Kathleen wants to talk to you." He glanced down at the blond girl beside him. "Come on, let's get out of here."

Palmer grabbed Kathleen's arm. "Wait a minute, Kathy. You said we could talk later. Why don't you get rid of this jerk and I'll take you for a ride in my convertible?"

Ellie could almost feel the anger growing in Jesse. His muscles tensed and she knew he was preparing to fight. Moving quickly toward the group, she said loudly, "Is that the convertible your grannie bought you because you finally made higher than an F in college?"

Luke Owens's laughter drowned out the snickers from the others in the room, but Ellie could only see the spark of amused approval in Jesse's eyes as he and Kathleen turned to leave the diner.

"Are you saying I'm stupid?" Palmer asked, turning his frustration on Ellie.

She smiled. "I didn't exactly say that. All I'm saying is that anyone who fails music appreciation *twice* just ain't too burdened with the smarts."

"At least I'm going to college," Palmer said, his face turning bright red at being the object of the growing laughter. "That creep never even made it out of high school."

Ellie's eyes narrowed angrily. "He had to support himself and his daddy," she said, her voice tight. "If you had that kind of responsibility, Palmer Catlin, you'd crawl in a corner and whine."

"That's telling him, Ellie," Luke said, giving Palmer a triumphant glance.

"Oh shut up, Luke," she hissed and turned her back on them both.

"You bitch," Luke said in a low voice, grabbing her arm. Then when he looked up and saw Sid watching closely, he dropped her arm and turned back to his friends.

Ellie went back to her seat, but jealousy was eating her alive. She couldn't think of anything other than Jesse and Kathleen. Where were they now? Would they go parking again? Would Jesse kiss her, touch her?

Ellie couldn't stand envisioning the scene that loomed before her eyes. She began to massage her temples, trying to relieve the tension, but it was no use. The noise in the diner began to close in on her.

Standing abruptly, she walked to the counter. "Sid," she called over the noise of the dishwasher, "I don't think I'll wait for you to get off work. I feel like walking."

"You know your Grannie Jean doesn't want you walking around after dark."

He started to move toward her, but she waved him away. "She won't know about it."

"Ellie, don't," he protested. "Just wait until my next break and I'll take you."

She shook her head stubbornly and left, ignoring him when he called her name again.

Outside the air was warm and heavy. Maybe walking would clear her mind. Grannie Jean always told her envy was a sin. If she was right, Ellie was headed straight for hell because she envied Kathleen with every bone in her body.

If only she had blond hair and big breasts. If only she looked like a delicate rose instead of sturdy Johnson grass. Then maybe Jesse would see her as a woman instead of the little girl he had gotten out of scrapes. He might as well be her brother, she thought in disgust.

Leaving the lighted square, she cut through the alley beside the five and dime, unconscious of the shadows cast by the streetlights that stretched and blurred until they merged with darkness. When a slight breeze rustled the dry weeds, she started to hurry forward then caught her breath sharply when a more solid hunk of darkness stepped away from the building directly in her path.

"Didn't anyone ever tell you not to walk around after dark, Ellie?"

The voice was no more than a rough whisper and for a moment she stood still in fear, then she let out an irritated breath.

"Luke Owens, what do you mean jumping out at me like that?" She moved closer to give him a heated look. "And what are you doing out here anyway? Did you follow me?"

"Why would I do that?" Ellie didn't like the smile she could hear in his husky voice. "You don't like me, remember?"

"That's what I'm wondering," she muttered and began to move around him. "Just go away and stop pestering me or I'll tell Jesse."

He grabbed her arm and jerked hard, throwing her off balance so that she fell against him. "I'm getting real tired of that threat, Ellie. I think it's time I showed you just how scared I am of Jesse Perkins."

He placed a rough hand behind her neck and pulled her forward. His lips found hers in a kiss that hurt and seemed to go on forever. The unpleasant taste of whiskey gagged her as his tongue tried to invade her mouth, but she kept her teeth clenched tightly, making angry noises in her throat. At last, she managed to jerk her lips away from his.

"Let go," she demanded harshly, kicking out at him. Her foot connected with his shin and he let out a harsh grunt, but before she could take advantage of his pain he swiftly twisted her around so that her back was to him and she could do no further damage.

She struggled frantically to free herself, but he held her in a firm grip, his forearm slung across her shoulders as he captured both her wrists with one large hand.

"Let me show you how scared I am, Ellie," he whispered in her ear as he brought his free hand to her chest and squeezed roughly on one breast.

"You bastard," she gasped. "Jesse will kill you for this."

His breathing quickened and when his hand slid down across her stomach, she knew what was coming and fought wildly. "I don't think so," he whispered, his voice raspy. "I think he's going to be too busy with the jet set to care what happens to you."

She couldn't let him touch her there. A blinding red fury exploded within her and, wrenching her arm free, she scratched viciously and deeply into his forearm. Even when he yelled and loosened his hold on her, she didn't let go. She was bent on sinking her nails into him and leaving a mark for the way he had touched her.

It was only when she heard laughter on the street that Ellie allowed Luke to sling her away from him against the wall. She didn't waste a precious second, but darted at once for Mr. Purley's field. Her breath came in harsh gasps as she ran through the night toward the safety of home.

Chapter Three

Jesse's eyes stayed on the road ahead, unconsciously taking in the dark shapes of the trees. Making his way down from the wooded hill on which Kathleen lived he could see the countryside for twenty miles around.

There were small pockets of light, wide spots really, in the distance that were towns, some containing not more than two or three hundred people. Jesse could name every one of the towns and knew most of the people in each. Some were smaller, some were larger than Bitter; but they were all the same kind of town inhabited by the same kind of people.

Jesse had passed by the same scenery hundreds of times, and tonight he took it all in without really seeing it. Instead, as he drove, he saw flirting blue eyes and pouting red lips.

Kathleen's teasing was driving him crazy. He tried to relax his tense shoulder muscles, wondering now how much longer he could take it. Every time they were together it was always the same. She would let him go just so far, then shut him off with promises for next time.

She kept insisting she was a virgin, with all a virgin's fears, but, though Jesse wanted very much to believe her, deeper instinct was beginning to ask how an innocent knew all the tricks designed specifically to make a man lose his cool.

Pulling a cigarette from a pack on the dashboard, he lit it with frustrated movements. However she managed it, an evening with Kathleen tore at his nerves. Jesse couldn't wait to get back to the Pixie, back to Ellie. He needed her directness right now.

He smiled as he thought of her straightforward personality. There was nothing coy about Ellie. His relationship with her was the one uncomplicated thing in his life. Sometimes Jesse thought that if Ellie weren't around to be his ground wire, he would lose touch with the person he really was. She knew and accepted what was inside him.

Suddenly a vision of Luke Owens invaded his thoughts and Jesse frowned in displeasure. He didn't like the way Luke had watched Ellie at the Pixie earlier in the evening, his gaze running over her breasts and legs as though she were on display especially for him.

Luke had no business hanging around her the way he was lately. The stocky troublemaker had always teased Ellie, but it was only recently that he had watched her with a gleam of desire in his eyes.

Jesse couldn't understand the way things were changing. Ellie had always detested Luke, but suddenly where Ellie was, Luke was there also. It just wasn't possible that she was encouraging him.

Or was it, he wondered grimly. Ellie was growing up fast. Maybe she had decided to test her burgeoning femininity on Luke?

The thought almost made him laugh. Ellie as a femme fatale was a little too much even for his imagination. She was too honest, too open to try those kinds of tricks, he assured himself.

But if he found out she was playing around with that kind of fire, he decided fiercely, he would dust her britches for her. Although Ellie could usually take care of herself just fine, she had no business fooling around with someone as wild and reckless as Luke.

Suddenly he smiled. She had looked like a pugnacious pussycat when she had jumped in and tackled Palmer earlier in the evening. To most people, Ellie seemed like a sweet little girl, but Jesse knew that when she was angry, it was time to take cover. He had discovered to his regret that she could fight like a wildcat.

Chuckling, he remembered the time she had left her teeth marks in his hand. He still had the scar. And all for a dog, he thought ruefully. Ellie had a habit of picking up any stray that needed a home.

Jesse could remember when Grannie Jean's small house had habitually harbored five or six animals at a time. Dogs, cats, and once a wild raccoon—anything that Ellie felt needed her was taken in. That situation hadn't lasted. Before long Grannie Jean had put her foot down. And Ellie's menagerie had dwindled to only two black cats and a skinny spotted dog.

Jesse braked sharply as he saw the eyes of a possum shining red in the headlights. The action effectively brought his concentration back to the road before him. The landscape had flattened out, and he could see the lights of Bitter rising above the highway ahead.

Whenever Jesse left town, even for a short drive, he always felt anxiety building in him as he drew closer. Every nerve tensed, and a hard pressure grew in his chest. It was as though for a brief while he had been a free man, only to be forced to return to prison. The prison was all the more hellish for existing only in his mind. He hated the feeling and fought it constantly. If it hadn't been for Ellie he would have left years before.

No, that was wrong, he thought as honesty forced its way to the surface. He wouldn't have left his father. There were times when he thought if he couldn't get away from Daryl Perkins he would scream. But Jesse knew he wouldn't leave, not as long as his father needed him.

He exhaled slowly, forcing his muscles to relax. He had to forget the bad, because now there was Kathleen. He needed no other excuse to keep him in Bitter. Since he had been seeing her, the town hadn't seemed so much of a pain in his gut. Being with Kathleen made him seem almost respectable. He enjoyed watching the same expression on the faces of the people who saw him with Mr. Dowe's only daughter. It was not only surprise but doubt, as though maybe they had misjudged him. Yes, he liked that feeling.

Approaching Bitter from the direction of The Hill, there were only a couple of outlying houses, and Jesse came upon the town suddenly. He passed through the small town square and drove on to the Pixie, pulling his truck into the gravel driveway. With only a couple of cars in front, the drive-in looked deserted.

He glanced at his watch. Ten forty-five. Sid would be getting off in fifteen minutes.

Inside Jesse found Sidney cleaning the grill under the watchful eye of Mrs. Higgins. There were still a few stragglers in the dining room, but a quick glance told Jesse that Ellie was not among them.

"Hey, Sid," he called. "Where's Ellie?"

Sid turned his head but continued to work as he spoke. "She got antsy and left."

Jesse's brow creased and a frown crossed his features. "You mean she walked home? How long ago was that?"

"About an hour." Sid shook his head. "I tried to stop her, but you know how Ellie is."

"Damn," Jesse said under his breath. "I'll tan her hide. She knows she's not supposed to be walking around after dark." He moved his shoulder muscles wearily then turned toward the door. "I'll see you later, Sid."

Pushing the door open, he started toward his truck, then suddenly his steps slackened. Luke Owens was leaning against the door of Jesse's blue pickup.

Jesse's eyes widened slightly in surprise. Luke must have been doing some pretty heavy drinking. He didn't usually challenge Jesse. Luke's courage worked best on people smaller than himself.

Walking over to the truck, he eyed the shorter man with resigned expectancy. "You want to get out of my way, Luke?" he asked softly.

"Not really," Luke said, smiling.

Jesse heard muffled laughter coming from the shadows beside the drive-in. It explained a lot. Luke had apparently decided to show all his friends he was tough enough to take on Jesse Perkins.

Jesse's evening had been a tense one, and he was in no mood to play stupid games with a drunk. He wanted to go home and think about all that had happened. Grabbing Luke's shirt with one hand, he shoved him aside, then opened the door of the pickup.

Luke leaned against the bed of the truck, eyeing Jesse. "You seem kinda touchy. Whatsa matter, Jesse?" he said, his speech slurred, his grin wide. "Didn't you get none?" He stepped closer to speak in what he must have intended to be a confiding whisper. "You should have stayed around here. I had better luck."

Jesse inhaled deeply, his gaze trained on the sky for a moment, impatience evident in his stance. "Have you got something to say, Luke?"

"Me?" The other man laughed, again darting a glance toward the corner where his friends were hidden, making sure they were enjoying the entertainment he was providing. "I was just saying that there was probably more action here than there was up on The Hill."

"What kind of action?" Jesse asked. Luke wasn't going to let it go until he had said what he had come to say.

"Now, Jesse," he said. "Do I look like the kind who tells tales out of school?" He started to walk away, then, over his shoulder, he added softly, "Ellie's really growing up, isn't she?"

Jesse froze. For a moment there was no reaction, then he felt anger rip through him. But along with it, almost hidden by it, was fear. Nothing could happen to Ellie. Before Luke had taken two steps away, Jesse grabbed his arm, swinging him around violently.

"What in hell are you talking about?" Jesse whispered hoarsely.

Luke shook off Jesse's hand and moved away from him toward his friends. "Come on, Jesse. Don't tell me you haven't sampled a little yourself," he asked, his voice taunting. "She's one... hot...chick."

When Luke grinned, Jesse knew he was waiting for an explosion. But Jesse didn't speak. His dark eyes blazed as he moved slowly toward the other man.

Luke licked his lips nervously and began to back away. "Listen, Jesse," he said. "You don't own Ellie. If she wants to get it on with me, then you don't have anything to say about it."

"I think you're making it all up," Jesse said softly. "But if you're not. If you laid one finger on Ellie, you'll be sorry for it, Luke."

Luke glanced toward his friends in the shadows then back at Jesse. He couldn't back down in front of his peers. In his group it wasn't allowed. "You can't tell me what to do," he said defiantly.

Luke reached up to push his hair off his forehead and when he did, Jesse saw the marks on his arm. They went deep and were red and angry looking.

Jesse stopped abruptly and stared at the wound. Before he consciously pieced together the facts, he felt a white-hot burst of fury explode inside his head. *"You son of a bitch!"* he roared.

Rushing forward he savagely threw his shoulder into Luke's middle. When he caught the stocky man off guard, they fell together on the gravel, each intent on doing damage to the other.

Minutes later Jesse was straddling Luke, drawing back to hit him again, when he felt someone grab him from behind. He struggled wildly when Sid held his arms and began to pull him off Luke.

"Jesse, Jesse," Sid said calmly, shaking his head in disapproval. "I can't take you anywhere, can I? Whatcha want to hit old Luke for? Hasn't anyone ever told you to be kind to dumb animals?"

Jesse was bent over at the waist, trying to catch his breath. Straightening at last, he wiped the blood from his mouth, then glanced around. Luke had disappeared along with his friends.

"That bastard," he said, his voice still rough, "has been messing with Ellie."

Sid's face went deathly still, then he exploded with a string of vulgarities that impressed even Jesse. When they heard a car start on the other side of the Pixie, Sid jerked around. But before he had taken two steps the car erupted onto the street, swerving crazily then straightening just as it disappeared from sight.

Sid slapped his fist against his thigh in frustrated anger. "I knew he'd been watching her lately," he said harshly. He fell silent for a tense moment. "I'll catch him," he said quietly. "I'll catch him sometime when he's not expecting me." He smiled in a way that was not pleasant, then he glanced back at Jesse. "How'd you find out?"

The fight had drained some of Jesse's anger, and he laughed softly. "I saw her scratch marks on his arm. You know that trick of hers. She'll fake you out then calmly bare her claws."

Sid chuckled.

"The little wildcat. I'm going to kick her butt for walking around after dark," Jesse said, grinning.

Sid straightened his back in a tired gesture. "You'll have to wait in line," he said, then began to walk away. "I'll see you, Jesse."

"See you, Sid."

Jesse stood quietly as he watched Sid's old Chevy pull away. Then he reached up to touch the cut on his lip. It had begun to sting. Suddenly from behind him came the sound of low laughter. He turned slowly to see Palmer moving out from behind several garbage cans into the light.

"Tsk, tsk," Palmer said, shaking his head. "You don't look too cool and calm now, Jesse. That's a nasty temper you've got." He smiled. "You'd better watch it. It just might get you into trouble one of these days."

Jesse swore silently. He had had enough for one night. Palmer was just exactly who he didn't need to see right now. "Is there something you wanted, Palmer? Or are you just naturally attracted to garbage cans?"

"That's very funny," he said, trying to sound as though he were amused by the insult. "You won't be laughing when Uncle John proves that you messed with those band instruments." He smiled. "Going to jail will only be the beginning. When he gets through with you, you won't have a job."

"Do I look scared? Your uncle knows what he can do with his job. I don't need it."

When Palmer frowned, Jesse knew what was going through his mind. Like Luke, Palmer got a kick out of intimidating people. But where Luke did it with muscle, Palmer did it with power. He enjoyed being a rich man's heir.

Only Jesse didn't intimidate so easily. He was more likely to be amused, and his confidence was like a thorn in Palmer's side. Jesse was white trash. Everyone in the county knew that. He should have been cowed, or at least disturbed, by the power Palmer wielded.

"And just how do you think you're going to support your father without your job at the pits?" he asked, giving a nasty laugh. "Because it's for damn sure he's not going to support himself."

"You can leave my father out of this," Jesse said, his voice soft.

Anyone with discretion would have heeded the warning. But Palmer was too angry to be discreet. He had to get the better of Jesse, just once.

He was silent for a moment, his eyes calculating as he glanced up at the sky then back to Jesse. "You didn't know that Uncle John went to see your old man tonight, did you?" he said, smiling. "While you were out pretending to be somebody with Kathleen."

Every muscle in Jesse's body tensed. He wanted to grab Palmer by the throat, but he knew that was the reaction the other man was waiting for. Clenching his fists, Jesse held his silence.

"He wanted to see if your daddy knew anything about where you were last night," Palmer continued. He eyed Jesse's tightly clenched fists and laughed. "He should have known the old drunk would be too soused to make sense."

Bending down, Jesse picked up a pebble and began tossing it in the air. Jesse wanted to shake Palmer and make him tell what had happened. He knew that the blond man would drag it out just to make Jesse sweat.

Palmer continued. "Have you ever seen my uncle get mad?" he shook his head ruefully. "It's not nice, to say the least. He never gets mad—never shouts, but his words cut deep. Real deep,'' he added, his voice quiet as though he were remembering. "He can make you feel like he's stripping the skin off you inch by inch.''

"Get on with it, Catlin,'' Jesse rasped.

"Uncle John got mad tonight.'' He inhaled. "He enjoyed telling me about it. He even laughed.'' Palmer shook his head. He had started this with the intention of hurting, but now he looked slightly confused as though his uncle's actions scared even him. "When your daddy wouldn't say anything except what a 'good boy' you are, Uncle John got mad. He just happened to let slip the fact that he had slept with your mama before she left town.''

Jesse felt bile rising in his throat. His head felt as though it were about to burst from some intolerable pressure inside it. He couldn't think, but instinctively, he knew he had to get away. He had to shut them all out. The rest of Palmer's words came to him through a red haze.

"He laughed, Jesse,'' Palmer whispered, his eyes narrowed as he stepped closer. "When your daddy started to cry, Uncle John laughed.''

"Shut up!" He shoved Palmer back into the garbage cans, the noise sounding explosive. "Just shut up, you bastard!'' Blood was pounding in his head, causing his vision to blur. "I'll kill him,'' he whispered, turning back to the blue pickup. "I'll kill him for this.''

Slowly Palmer pulled himself up and leaned against the wall of the Pixie, dodging as Jesse spun out of the driveway, the tires throwing gravel wildly.

Ellie felt a hand on her shoulder, shaking her awake. Rubbing a hand across her eyes drowsily, she found Grannie Jean bending over her. Grannie's hair was in a long braid down her back, and her faded chenille robe was wrapped around her tightly. Someone had gotten her out of bed.

"Grannie?" she asked, her voice husky with sleep as she sat up.

"Chief Sharpe is here, Ella Mae," Grannie said brusquely. "He wants to talk to you."

It was a moment before Ellie took in what the older woman was saying, then her heart began to pound. Scrambling from bed, she pulled on the knee-length cotton robe her grandmother held for her.

"It's Jesse, isn't it?" she whispered.

Her grandmother nodded silently, her features even sterner than usual.

"Is he hurt, Grannie Jean? Was he driving too fast again?" She reached out to clutch the older woman's arm. "Did he have a wreck?"

"Jesse's not hurt," Grannie Jean said. "You come on in the living room and let that idiot...let the chief tell you about it."

Her mouth was dry with fear as she followed Grannie into the living room. Grampa was there, too. He had pulled on loose-fitting khaki trousers, and a ribbed white undershirt exposed his thin shoulders and chest. He looked vulnerable. A man like Chief Sharpe shouldn't be allowed to make her grandfather look vulnerable.

The head of Bitter's police force stood by the front door. Reluctantly Ellie walked toward him, her eyes wide with fear. She stopped several feet in front of him and waited silently for the ax to fall.

"Ella Mae," he said, and his voice sounded unnaturally loud in the small, familiar room. "Somebody tried to rob Mr. Catlin tonight."

Ellie caught her breath. She nodded slowly and waited for him to continue. But in her heart, she knew what was coming next.

"He was working late at his office when it happened. Whoever did it hurt him real bad. He's in the hospital with head injuries." He glanced away from her terrified eyes. "We're looking for Jesse."

Although he had said the words quietly, they rang wildly in Ellie's ears. "He didn't," she whispered desperately. "He didn't do it." She reached out in supplication, then let her hand fall. "Jesse wouldn't hurt anyone," she said, her voice urgent. "You know he wouldn't." She turned to stare at her grandparents. "Grannie Jean...Grampa, tell him. Jesse wouldn't hurt anyone."

Her grandfather stepped forward to put his arm around Ellie. Grannie Jean glared at Chief Sharpe. "What is it you want from my granddaughter, Tom? You didn't get her out of bed just to scare her to death."

"No, ma'am, Miz Cooper," he said politely. "I want to know if she's seen Jesse since she left the Pixie. Nobody seems to know where he is. His daddy hasn't seen him since he left for the dance."

Ellie tried desperately to think. Where was Jesse? she wondered frantically. Why wasn't he home? She had never been so scared. This felt different from all the other times he had been in trouble.

Moistening her lips in a nervous gesture, she shook her head. "I haven't seen him, Chief Sharpe. But he didn't do it," she added hastily. "I know he didn't do it."

"Ella Mae, Jesse started a fight with Luke Owens around eleven tonight," Sharpe said sternly. "For no reason. He was just looking for trouble like he usually does."

"Luke Owens!" Grannie snorted in disbelief. "Luke Owens wouldn't know the truth if it reached out and tapped him on the shoulder." She stared hard at Sharpe. "And if he wasn't your cousin Tyla's boy you'd admit it."

The redfaced man looked uncomfortable for a moment, then he cleared his throat. "The part about Luke doesn't really matter. It just indicates what kind of mood Jesse was in tonight. The real evidence comes from Palmer Catlin. He heard Jesse threaten his uncle."

"Threaten him?" Ellie asked in confusion. "What do you mean?"

"He said he would kill him. Then he left the Pixie. That was a little after eleven. Mr. Catlin's watch stopped at fifteen until twelve."

The silence in the room was deafening as Chief Sharpe turned to leave at last. "I know Jesse's your friend, Ella Mae," he added as he reached the door. "But we're talking about the law here. If you see him or hear from him, you have to get in touch with me. It's your duty."

When the door closed behind him, Ellie swung around. She couldn't keep pace with her chaotic thoughts. She couldn't calm down enough to think what to do. Except that she knew she had to find Jesse.

Glancing up, she found her grandparents watching her, sympathy filling their eyes. "I've got to find him," she whispered.

Grannie Jean shook her head. "There isn't anything you can do for Jesse now, Ella Mae. And it's too late for you to go traipsing around town. You go get back in bed; you're starting to shiver."

It wasn't the night air that was making her shiver. She stared at her grandmother, words of argument on her lips, then she sighed. It was no use. Once Grannie Jean had made up her mind there was no changing it.

"You do like your Grannie says," her grandfather said. "Come give me a hug then get back in bed."

She put her arms around his neck and kissed his cheek. Before she could pull away, he whispered, "Be sure and push the screen back in when you leave, sweetheart."

"Oh, Grampa," she said, her voice unsteady with suppressed emotion. "I love you."

"Go on, now. Go to bed."

She turned toward her bedroom. "Good night, Grannie Jean. Good night, Grampa."

"Good night, Ella Mae."

She waited until the springs stopped creaking in her grandparents' room, then she slipped from the bed. Her hands were shaking as she quickly pulled on her clothes, urgency building with each passing second.

When she was dressed, she unlatched the screen and pushed it outward then slipped quietly through the window. The second her feet touched the ground outside, she was running. She knew where to go to find him. When Jesse was brooding or hurt, he went to the cabin. It was the one place where no one could touch him.

She ran through the dark, never once stopping for breath, unmindful of the branches that pulled at her clothes and arms. She didn't pause when she burst into the clearing, but stumbled toward the small structure.

Throwing open the door, she said, "Jesse!" intending the word to be a scream but having only the strength for a breathless whisper.

Appearing from the darkness, he grabbed her arm and swung her around to face him. "What is it? Ellie, what's wrong?" He put his arms around her trembling body. "My God, you're white as a ghost."

"Jesse," she rasped. "Oh, Jesse."

"Stop it," he soothed. "Everything's all right. I'm here now."

Ellie would have laughed if she hadn't felt so much like crying. He was taking care of her like he always did. "Jesse, something terrible's happened."

"What?" He grasped her shoulders and held her away from him. "It's not Luke, is it? God, I'll kill that bastard if he—"

She shook her head frantically. "It's not Luke. It's Mr. Catlin." Her chest hurt like crazy. She was trying to catch her breath and tell him at the same time. "He's been hurt. Someone—someone hurt him." She clutched at his arm. "Jesse, they think it was you. Chief Sharpe came to the house. He said—he said..."

Jesse had gone still when she mentioned John Catlin, now he pulled her down to sit beside him on the old cot. "What did he say?"

His voice sounded strange and terror shot through her. She whispered, "He said Palmer heard you threaten to kill Mr. Catlin. Did you, Jesse?"

He ran his fingers through his hair then gave her a wry look. "Yes, I guess I did."

She moaned, wrapping her arms tightly around his waist. "It's trouble this time, Jesse. I just know it." She glanced up, her eyes pleading. "You've got to have an alibi. You've got to prove you were some-where else, that you didn't go near Palmer's uncle."

"But I did."

The softly spoken words were like a shout in the dark room. Ellie felt her heart come to a complete stop. When it started again, it raced frantically. She tried to speak, but no words came out.

Jesse stood up, rubbing the back of his neck with both hands. "I went to see him right after I left Pal-mer at the Pixie." He shrugged his shoulders and the movement looked strangely awkward. "Ellie, I had to. Palmer told me his uncle went to my house to-night and...and said things to my father." He ex-haled a harsh breath. "But it wasn't just because of what he said. It was because—God, what he did was like kicking a dog or—or hurting a baby. He attacked—he was cruel to someone who was unable to defend himself.''

He swung around to stare at her passionately. "I couldn't let him get away with it. You see that, don't you? I had to make him understand that what he had done was wrong. No . . . no, it was evil.''

"You don't have to make excuses to me," she said softly, earnestly.

He smiled. "I know. But I need to tell you about it." He inhaled slowly. "I was mad as fire when I left the Pixie after talking to Palmer. I didn't even stop to think. I drove straight to Mr. Catlin's office. I knew sometimes he worked at the office on Saturday nights.''

"What happened?" she asked reluctantly.

He shrugged. "Nothing really, except a nasty exchange of insults. I guess I knew before I got there that he wouldn't listen to me, that what I said wouldn't make any difference, but I had to try anyway.''

"Of course you did," she said loyally. "What time did you leave his office?"

"I think it was around eleven-thirty." His smile was ironic. "It didn't take long to figure out that I was wasting my breath.''

She sat forward eagerly. "Then the night watchman should be able to clear you.''

He shook his head. "He can tell them what time I got there because he let me in . . .'' When he paused, she held her breath. "But I didn't see him when I left."

She almost moaned. Everything was conspiring to make him look guilty. "Wasn't there anyone on the street who could have seen you leave the building?"

"Nobody we could question." At her glance of inquiry, he said, "When I got to the street, someone was messing with my truck." He shook his head. "I yelled and he ran away. It was too dark to see who it was."

She remained silent for a moment, then suddenly she stood up. "You've got to leave town," she said, her voice steady and determined now. "You've got to go somewhere where they can't find you."

"Ellie, that's dumb." He stood up, too, frowning down at her. "I can't run away."

"Yes, you can," she said stubbornly. "Jesse, this is different from all the other times. This time they'll send you to jail for sure. I just know it." She started to pace. "You can't go back to your house. They would catch you. You'll just have to—"

"Peanut, listen to me."

"I'll take care of your daddy for you. And you can let me know where you are so I—"

He grabbed her arms and shook her hard. "Stop it!"

She blinked several times then stared up at him as though coming awake.

He gazed down at her for a moment, then said softly, "Ellie, I didn't do it."

She smiled. "I know that." She reached up to touch his face. "I know you could never do anything bad. I never thought for a minute that you hurt Mr. Catlin." She shrugged. "But what I know doesn't count. Everyone else will think you did it. You have to leave until Mr. Catlin gets better."

"I can't run away." He frowned. "Don't you see? If I run away then they've won. I'll be as good as admitting I did it. I've got to stay and prove I didn't."

She gazed up at him. The moonlight struck his lean face, highlighting the strong lines. She couldn't let anything happen to Jesse. "I'm afraid," she whispered suddenly.

He pulled her close and laughed huskily. "So am I," he said. He began to walk with her toward the door. "But it'll work out all right. You just wait and see."

He opened the door and they stepped out. Then he stopped suddenly as though he had just remembered something. "Ellie, about Luke—I ran into him tonight."

Ellie glanced away from him, but he caught her chin and lifted her eyes to his. "What happened?"

She shrugged casually. "It was nothing. You know how Luke is. He'd been drinking and was just trying to throw his weight around." She grinned suddenly. "I don't think he'll bother me again."

He chuckled. "I noticed that nice work you did on his arm."

She laughed unsteadily, then moved closer to him. "Jesse, what's going to happen?" she whispered, her gray eyes frightened.

He stared up at the stars for a moment, then exhaled. "I don't know. I guess I'd better go and find out."

They began to walk slowly away from the cabin.

Chapter Four

Ellie stared down at her oatmeal, running her spoon listlessly through the gray mass. Her appetite had deserted her, and she knew she wouldn't regain it until she found out if Jesse was all right.

It was Sunday morning, which meant she was wearing her Sunday dress—the green one with the wide white belt—but if she didn't hear something from Jesse soon, Ellie had decided she would skip church and go find him, no matter what Grannie Jean said.

After they had left the cabin the night before, Ellie had begged Jessie to let her go with him to confront the police, but he had remained stubborn in his refusal, sending her home to bed. She hadn't slept. She hadn't even tossed and turned. She had merely stared out the window, watching the attic fan suck unwary bugs against the window screen. Never in her short life had she felt so helpless.

"If there were lumps in that oatmeal, I believe you've taken care of them."

Ellie looked up to find her grandmother watching her closely. The older woman's long brown hair was caught up in a net at the back of her head, and she was wearing her navy blue dress with white carnations spreading geometrically across the dark cotton cloth. Her other Sunday dress was navy with pale pink roses.

Ellie sighed heavily. "I'm sorry, Grannie Jean. I told you I wasn't hungry."

"And I told you it wouldn't help Jesse none to have you starve yourself," she said, her voice stern, her sharp eyes concerned as she moved to the table and picked up the still full bowl. "Eat your toast, then you can go find out what's happening to him."

Ellie's smile showed her relief and gratitude. She forced herself to take a bite of the cold toast. It felt dry and heavy in her mouth. Swallowing a hasty gulp of milk to help it go down, she grimaced and then glanced up sharply when she heard a knock at the front door. In her haste to stand, she almost knocked over the chair.

"Sit down," Grannie Jean said. "Your grampa will get the door."

"But—"

"*Sit!*"

"Yes, ma'am."

They both turned when Grampa walked into the room with Sidney. "Morning, Mrs. Cooper," the younger man said. "Morning, Ellie."

Ellie could stay in her chair no longer. She jumped up and ran to Sid, clasping his upper arm between anxious hands, her eyes searching his face. "What's happened, Sid? What did they do to him? Is he all right?"

"Ella Mae," her grandmother said sternly. "That's enough." She wiped her hands on a dish-cloth as she turned to Sid. "Good morning, Sidney. How's your baby sister? Is that cold still bothering her?"

"She's just fine now, Mrs. Cooper," he answered, his voice polite. "She's still got a little cough, but the fever's all gone."

How could Sid stand being so patient? Ellie wondered in frustration. She knew by the way he kept his dark eyes trained on her face that he had something urgent to tell her, but there was a ritual that grown-ups went through when they met and apparently Sidney had already graduated into that exasperating category.

"Tell us about Jesse," Grannie Jean said at last, pointedly ignoring Ellie's sigh of relief. "Do you know what's happened to him?"

"They arrested him."

As her knees gave way, Ellie sank weakly to the chair behind her. Her eyes darted frantically around the room, searching for something stable to hold on to. She felt Grampa's hands on her shoulders and turned to him. "Grampa?" she whispered. "What can we do?"

He glanced up, his gaze seeking his wife. Slowly, irresistibly, Sid and Ellie turned to face her as well.

"How's Mr. Catlin doing this morning?" Grannie asked, her expression thoughtful. "Has he come to yet?"

Sid shook his head. "They won't tell me much, but they did say he was still unconscious."

Grannie Jean's eyes narrowed the way Grampa's did when the smoke from his pipe got in his eyes. "Well then, first thing we've got to do," Grannie said calmly, "is see how bad their case against Jesse is...what kind of evidence they've got and such. Then we need to see about a lawyer so we can get him out of jail."

Unreasonably they all felt better. She had given them a direction. The four of them sat down together at the kitchen table to discuss it.

"Sidney, do you know what they used to arrest Jesse?" Grannie asked.

Sid rubbed his chin, his expression rueful. "The fact that Palmer heard him threaten Mr. Catlin and the fact that the night watchman let him in before midnight but didn't see him leave."

"Was Jesse the only one who went into the building?" This came from Grampa.

Sid shrugged. "I don't know if they even asked."

Grannie Jean shook her head doubtfully. "Probably not," she said in disgust. "Tom Sharpe is determined to get Jesse for something." She moved her shoulders as if they ached. "In fact, I can think of a lot of people in this town who would like to see Jesse put away."

The four people around the table each added to that thought, naming people—influential people— who hated Jesse because he didn't conform. People were named who despised him because they felt he looked down on them when he wasn't entitled to. And people who feared him because he saw the decay beneath their surface respectability.

"So what about a lawyer?" Grannie Jean said at last, breaking the silence.

"He's got a court-appointed lawyer," Sidney said. "A man named Marshall."

Grannie nodded. "That's good. Mr. Perkins doesn't have money for a lawyer and neither do we." She frowned. "Has anyone told Mr. Perkins?"

Sid shook his head, his eyes wary. "I was going to go there next."

He didn't have to tell anyone it was a task he dreaded. Daryl Perkins tended to become emotional at even inconsequential things. This news about his son would devastate him.

"You stay here and have some breakfast," Grannie said firmly as she stood and removed her apron. "Ralph and I will go talk to him."

He nodded, his eyes grateful. As soon as her grandparents walked out of the kitchen, Ellie turned to Sid. "You're worried about the lawyer," she said. "Why?"

He shook his head. "I don't know, Ellie. Maybe I'm looking for trouble, but he's new and he's from up north. He's only been in Bitter for a couple of weeks, and I just don't think he understands how this town feels about Jesse."

He rested his forearms on the table, worry lines creasing his high forehead. "Other than his daddy, you and me and your grandparents are the only ones who care what happens to him." He paused, frowning. "The others are either not interested or they're too afraid of the Catlins and Tom Sharpe to say anything."

Acknowledging the truth of what he had said, she fell silent. After a couple of minutes of deep thought, she stood up. "I'm going to see this northern lawyer—this Mr. Marshall," she said, her chin held high, her eyes determined. "I'm going to tell him what's going on and make sure he tries to do something about it."

Sidney pushed back his chair and stood. "I'll go with you."

She shook her head. "You can't. This is Sunday." On the Sabbath when everyone else rested, Sidney cleaned the rest rooms and floors of the Wash'n'Dry Laundromat.

"That doesn't matter."

"It does, too. If you don't show up Mr. Atkins will fire you, and you'll never save the money for college." He started to continue the protest, but she stopped him. "I can do it by myself," she said quietly. "But if he won't listen to me, you can see him this evening."

Reluctantly, he acquiesced and started toward the back door. After pulling it open, he glanced back at her. "I suppose he'll be at home today. He's the one who rented old Mrs. Dobbs's place."

Ellie nodded, then walked to the counter to leave a note for her grandparents. Grannie would be upset about her missing church, but after all, she had almost given her permission. And Ellie simply couldn't continue her life as though nothing had happened.

As soon as she left the house, she cut through the yard of the house directly across the street. Mrs. Dobbs's place was three streets over. Ellie had visited it often with Grannie Jean before Mrs. Dobbs had passed away that spring. In her will, the elderly woman had left her house and furnishings to a cousin in San Antonio who was renting it out until he could get to Bitter to dispose of the property.

As she walked, Ellie nervously wiped her hands on her dress. What if the lawyer wouldn't see her? She was all primed to see him. It would be awful if he just turned her away. She could stand being made to feel insignificant, but what if he was a cold sort of person who didn't care what happened to Jesse?

Stop it, she told herself sternly. She had to remember what Jesse always said—don't look for trouble, it'll always find you without any problem at all.

That thought held her for about two and a half minutes, then she frowned. What if Mr. Marshall was at church? She hadn't even considered the possibility. If he was gone, she told herself, then she would simply sit on his doorstep until he returned.

When she spotted the house, she paused without thinking. The small frame structure had changed in the four months since Mrs. Dobbs's death. The once-neat yard had grown ragged, not enough to look neglected, just enough to look sad. And the paint on the window frames had begun to peel. One of the window screens had a small tear. There was nothing major wrong; it simply looked as though the house was mourning the death of Sally Dobbs.

Ellie mounted the front porch, her gaze avoiding the ivy that was turning brown in several hanging baskets. Drawing in a deep breath, she raised her fist and knocked on the door, hesitantly at first and then more firmly.

A muffled crash came from inside the house, then an oath; then there was silence. None of this was exactly encouraging, and Ellie was fidgeting impatiently from foot to foot when the door was opened at last.

She stared wide-eyed as she got her first glimpse of Jesse's lawyer. Thick glasses sat askew about a pale, whisker-stubbled face. He looked barely awake as he peered around the half-opened door at her.

"Cookies," he mumbled incomprehensibly.

When she stared at him in confusion, he straightened his glasses and said slowly, "It ought to be against the law to sell cookies on Sunday." Leaning against the doorjamb, he closed his eyes as a yawn stretched his features. "Okay," he said after a moment. "How much?"

"Mr. Marshall?" Ellie said tentatively.

He opened one eye. "Mmmm?" he replied sleepily.

"I'm Ellie Cooper and I'm not selling cookies."
Ellie decided she would talk Grannie Jean into making her a new Sunday dress if it was the last thing she ever did. "I'm here to talk to you about Jesse Perkins, sir."

He straightened and backed away from the door. "Perkins? The boy who was arrested last night?"

"He's twenty-two," she said defensively. "That's not a boy."

He smiled. "I wasn't trying to insult him. At my age, anyone under thirty is a child." He opened the door wider. "Come on in."

She stared at him in curiosity as she passed. He wasn't a large man, but he looked strong and wore yellow pajamas with little black horses and little brown men romping all over them. It suddenly occurred to her that she was alone with a man in his nightwear. But who could be afraid of a man with cowboys on his pajamas?

"You don't look that much older than Jesse," she said bluntly.

"But I am," he said as though he regretted the fact. "I'm thirty-five, and in law that's considered ancient to be just starting out."

After motioning toward a chair, he moved quickly to pull a bundle of clothes and several magazines off it so she could sit down.

"Now then," he said briskly as soon as Ellie was seated. "What can I do for you? Do you have some evidence that will help Perkins?"

She shifted uncomfortably under his scrutiny, then said, "No, I just wanted to know what you're doing about his arrest. Because Jesse didn't do what they say he did." She leaned forward, eager in her attempt to convince. "He's innocent, Mr. Marshall."

He studied her earnest face for a moment, then said, "Were you with Jesse when Mr. Catlin was attacked?"

For just a second Ellie considered lying, then she sighed and reluctantly shook her head.

He nodded, his expression pleased. "I'm glad you decided to tell the truth. I can't help your Jesse with lies."

That sounded encouraging. At least he was honest. "How are you going to help him?"

"Well, the first thing I'm going to do is try to convince the judge that there's not enough evidence to hold him over for trial." He shrugged. "But we have to wait for him to get back from a fishing trip."

"Judge Edwards?" she asked warily.

"Why do you say it like that?"

"Judge Edwards is Mr. Dowe's brother-in-law."

"I see. You make that sound very important. Who is Mr. Dowe?"

"He's Kathleen's father," she said portentiously.

He nodded slowly, his expression bewildered. "Well, that explains it." Then he leaned closer and said, "Who is Kathleen?"

"Jesse's girl," she said, unaware of how plainly her feelings showed on her expressive features.

He shot her a sympathetic glance. "I thought you were that."

"No, I'm just a friend." She waved an impatient hand. "That doesn't matter. What's important is Mr.

Dowe hates Jesse and Mr. Catlin is his business partner. Oh, and there's some kind of family tie. Cousins or something, which means the Catlins are also related to Judge Edwards . . . it's all a little confusing.''

"That sounds like an understatement,'' he said dryly. "From just the little you've told me, a good portion of Bitter should be cross-eyed and peabrained.''

When she merely stared at him, he shifted in his chair and crossed one knee over the other. "Never mind. That's just a weak attempt at humor. I'm good at weak humor,'' he added. "Now let me see if I've got this straight. You think Judge Edwards will be biased because he's Mr. Dowe's brother-in-law who is Mr. Catlin's business partner and distant relative.''

She nodded.

He leaned back in the chair, his thin face thoughtful as he rubbed his nose with his index finger. "You know that shouldn't make any difference to justice, don't you?''

Her expression spoke volumes in the ensuing silence.

"Okay,'' he said, smiling ruefully. "It shouldn't make any difference, but it could.''

"Not could, will,'' she said firmly. "It's not just all the family and business ties. Jesse's lived here all his life. And it's always been the same. Whenever there's any trouble, he gets blamed for it.''

"Why doesn't he leave?''

"He wants to, but his father won't go." Ellie thought of the way Mr. Perkins had always clung to the house in the hope that his wife would someday return. She shook her head slowly. "His father's... not well. Jesse has to stay and take care of him."

"Very admirable." He stood and paced several steps. "Look, Ellie. I think you can help me." He paused. "But I need the truth from you. You hesitated when you said Mr. Perkins is not well. What's the real story?"

Ellie frowned. It didn't seem right talking about Jesse's private business when he wasn't there. But she wanted desperately to help him and if this was the way to do it, then Ellie would swallow her scruples.

"Jesse's daddy is an alcoholic," she said slowly. "He started drinking real heavy when Jesse was twelve, and it's just gotten worse since then. Jesse had to quit school to support them both."

The lawyer whistled between his teeth. "Heavy," he muttered in sympathy. "What else?"

She glanced at him in inquiry.

"I need to know all the dirt. Anything that might affect a jury's opinion of Jesse."

Ellie inhaled deeply. "His mother left when he was twelve... that was when Mr. Perkins started drinking." She clenched her hands in her lap. "People say..."

"Go on," he urged. "What do they say?"

"Jesse says she was a whore," she said in a rush. "And once when I was behind a bush, hiding from Luke Owens, I heard Mrs. Wharton—her husband works at the tool and die factory—say that Mrs. Perkins had slept with just about everyone important in town. She said she—Mrs. Perkins—wouldn't fool around with anyone who couldn't give her a good time... you know, spend a lot of money on her." Ellie shrugged. "Mrs. Wharton seemed to think that was the only reason Mrs. Perkins hadn't gone after Mr. Wharton, but if you'd ever seen Mr. Wharton you'd know better."

He laughed in hearty enjoyment. "So what you're saying is that everyone in town is prejudiced against Jesse because of his parents?"

She considered the question for a moment then shook her head. "No. A lot of people like him. He's always helping people out. Old people or sick people. But those kind of people don't have any influence here." She frowned. "It's the others. They either remember his parents or they..."

"They what?" he prompted.

"It's hard to explain." Her brow creased as she tried to gather together the right words. "You've seen Jesse. Pretend you're a woman."

He glanced down at his pajamas. "If I were a woman I definitely wouldn't ask me for a date." When she gave him an exasperated look, he said, "Sorry. I think I know what you mean. I guess a woman would see Jesse as pretty sexy. All dark and brooding. Right?"

She nodded emphatically. "He seems to scare some women. The ones Grannie Jean calls mean spirited and pooh-pooh proper. She says if a man ever says howdeedo to them, they think he's trying to get in their drawers. And Grampa says if a man ever made the mistake of getting in their drawers, he'd leave right quick."

"I think I like your grandparents," he said, chuckling in genuine amusement.

Ellie found herself smiling, liking him against her will. "Grannie says hypocrites always get their just rewards because the Good Lord can tell which of his children knows the words to 'Leaning on the Everlasting Arms' and which ones are only moving their lips."

"My goodness, a philosopher. I never expected to find one in Bitter, Texas."

She shrugged. "I guess we've got just about everything they've got in the rest of the world. What we've got just doesn't move as fast."

He smiled. "I guess you do. And right now you've got just as much trouble as you'd find in a big city." He paused thoughtfully. "So Jesse's masculinity is a threat to frustrated women."

"Not to all of them. I see some of them watching him, like... Oh, I don't know. They get this weird look in their eyes. They pretend they disapprove of him, but their eyes wander over his chest and his legs like he was the bakery shop window or something." She shifted in her seat. "And I see their husbands watching them watch Jesse."

"Now we're getting to the heart of it." He walked to the fireplace and leaned against it, his arms crossed at his chest. "Yes, I see. I knew I sensed an atmosphere in the police station when I saw him last night. If a man were a little insecure about his own masculinity, someone like Jesse would be a natural scapegoat.''

She nodded, feeling a measure of relief. At least he was sharp enough to have recognized that there was a problem, even before she talked to him. ''So you see why he'll never get a fair trial here in Bitter?''

He nodded. ''If the evidence holds up and he's held over for trial, I'll try for a change of venue. But we have to depend on Mr. Catlin getting better before it comes to that. The officials are being very closemouthed about his condition, but I understand a specialist has been flown in from Houston.'' He smiled and shrugged. ''Who knows? Mr. Catlin may wake up today and make my job obsolete.''

He fell silent and suddenly Ellie knew he wasn't seeing her. His eyes were focused on something inside his head. After a moment he picked up a long yellow pad and began writing furiously.

''Mr. Marshall?'' she said when she began to grow impatient with his silence.

''Hmmm?'' He didn't look up.

''Couldn't I testify as a character witness at the arraignment?'' she asked.

He glanced up, then down at his pad, then up again. This time he saw her. ''I'm afraid not, honey,'' he said, shaking his head in regret. ''You're too young and besides, the judge will know how close you and Jesse are. Don't you worry; I believe Jesse's innocent. I thought so when I met him last night. Talking to you today has only confirmed that feeling.'' He smiled. ''Justice may be a little slow sometimes, but it doesn't allow for innocents to be punished for crimes they didn't commit."

When he began to write again, she sighed and stood up. He didn't notice when she left. As she walked toward the center of town Ellie went over everything she had learned. She liked Mr. Marshall. He was a little strange, but he seemed like a decent man. But she didn't know if he was capable of fighting Bitter. He had come onto the scene too late in the day to know the intricacies of life there. There was a kind of medieval protocol that had to be observed, a protocol that outsiders couldn't understand.

She had thought for a while that she was getting through to him, but the lawyer seemed positive Jesse would go free because he didn't know about the Catlins and the Dowes and the way they ran the county.

When she arrived at the small jail across the street from the courthouse, Ellie hesitated for only a moment, then she walked in.

Sitting behind a high counter opposite the door was a uniformed policeman. It was difficult for Ellie to remember that this was Frank Newbody who traded milk from his cows to Grannie Jean for fresh baked bread. He looked like a stranger in his brown uniform.

Glancing up from his newspaper, he smiled. Then all at once the smile faded, as though it had leaked out a hole in his chin, and his eyes narrowed. "Ella Mae, what are you doing here? This is no place for a little girl like you. Does your Grannie Jean know you're here?"

"I came to see Jesse, Mr. Newbody," she said, keeping her voice polite but firm.

He shook his head. "You go on home now. Your grannie would skin me alive if I let you into the jail."

"I want to see Jesse."

"Ella Mae," he said in exasperation. "We've got criminals back there. Men who don't respect innocence. Now you get on home where you belong."

Ellie kept her expression respectful, but she refused to budge. She would have stayed even if there had been real criminals in the jail. But she knew the jail cells contained no one more nefarious than a couple of nameless drifters and George Thompkins, waiting for his wife to pick him up after his usual Saturday night drinking spree.

"I want to see Jesse," she repeated for the third time. "I'm not leaving until I do."

Although he shook his head at her obstinancy, he reached behind him for a large round key ring. "You just wait in here." He opened the door to a small cluttered room. "The chief will probably have my hide, but I'll bring Jesse up here to see you." He winked at her. "I think I'd rather have the chief after me than your grannie."

Ellie stepped hesitantly inside the small room, glancing over her shoulder as he closed the door behind her. She looked around quickly then walked to the window. There were bars on it. She wondered if the person assigned to this dreary, airless office tried to escape often. Ellie knew she would if she had to work there.

When the door opened behind her, she swung around eagerly. Jesse walked in and stopped just inside the door as it closed behind him. At the sight of him, she felt her heart swell, filling her chest and intruding into her throat. She didn't know who took the first step, but a moment later she was held tightly in his arms.

It was a full minute before she could find her voice. "Oh, Jesse," she whispered. "I'm scared."

Without loosening his hold on her, he reached up to wipe away the tears that had spilled over onto her cheeks. "What's this?" he asked hoarsely.

"I'm not crying," she said, sniffing. "Did you think I was? I never cry."

"No, you don't." There was a strange, sad look on his face as he let his arms fall and stepped away from her. "You shouldn't have come here, Ellie. This is no kind of place for you."

She raised her chin stubbornly. "This is no kind of place for you, but you're here."

He laughed harshly. "Not by choice, believe me."

She studied his face trying to see into his thoughts, trying to share what he was feeling. But in some way he had closed her out.

"I talked to Mr. Marshall," she said, willing her misery not to show in her face.

One dark brow raised in inquiry. "What did you think of my Yankee mouthpiece?"

"I like him. He wears pajamas with cowboys on them."

"Oh, well, that makes me feel better," he said with wry humor. "How can I lose?"

She laughed. "I don't think he'll wear them in court. He seems...capable."

He shook his head. "I don't doubt his ability, but I'm a little worried about his naivete. If he thinks everything will go by the rules, he's in for a few surprises."

"I talked to him about that. About Judge Edwards and the Dowes and the Catlins."

He nodded. "Maybe he'll be all right. I hope so."

She inhaled, then forced a smile on her face. "Well, why are we acting so tragic, for heaven's sake. This is just a stupid mistake and you'll be out tomorrow, you'll see." She glanced around. "Besides I think it's kind of funky. I've never seen the inside of the jail before."

When he remained silent, she clasped his hand tightly, urging him to look at her. "Did you get an interesting roommate? Somebody who plays the harmonica and talks about going to the Big House?"

He smiled, reluctantly at first, then suddenly the smile grew. "I don't have a cell mate, but George Thompkins does a pretty fair rendition of 'Blue Suede Shoes.' Does that count?" he asked, hugging her close again. "You're right. There's no need to be so grim. I doubt I'll be out tomorrow, but sooner or later Mr. Catlin's going to tell them who did it. Then they'll have to let me go."

He stared down at her, his gaze tracing the signs of a sleepless night on her face. "I'm sorry you've been worried. I hate that you had to come here, that you've gone through this because of me."

She grinned. "It's only fair. After all, you stuck by me through puberty, didn't you?"

Laughing softly, he squeezed her shoulders and for a second she thought maybe everything would be all right. Then his face grew serious. "Have you seen Kathleen? Does she know—" he waved his arm around, indicating the bars on the window "—about all this?"

Ellie shrugged casually. "News doesn't get up to The Hill as fast as it gets around here," she said.

His dark eyes were worried as he walked to the window, his hands shoved in his back pockets. "I wish I could see her. This is such a mess. How can I expect her to understand when I don't understand it myself? I wish I could just talk to her and tell her... tell her that I'm innocent."

Ellie walked to him, hugging his arm to her breast, needing to touch him to reassure herself that he was safe. "She'll know you didn't do it, Jesse." It hurt as she said it. Every lying word hurt. "She cares about you."

His eyes met hers swiftly. "Do you think so?" he asked. His voice was carefully calm and free of emotion. But Ellie could see the anxiety in his dark eyes.

"Of course," she assured him. "Look, I'll go see her and tell her all about it. She'll probably be here to see you tomorrow."

He frowned. "No, tell her not to come. I don't want her to see me here." He walked to the cluttered desk. "I'll give you a note for her."

Bending over, he wrote hastily. There was barely enough time for him to hand her the note before Mr. Newbody returned to take Jesse back to his cell. Ellie bit her lip. She didn't want Jesse to see her cry again.

As he walked out the door, Jesse glanced back over his shoulder. "Check on Daddy for me, Ellie," he said quietly. "Will you?"

She ran to the door. "I'll take care of him, Jesse," she called down the hall. "Don't worry. I'll..." Her voice faded as a heavy door slammed behind him.

"I'll take care of everything," she whispered. Then she turned to leave.

Chapter Five

As soon as Sidney had finished his chores at the Laundromat, Ellie persuaded him to drive her up to The Hill to see Kathleen. Although it was only ten miles from town, the drive seemed to take them forever. The Hill was not a place Ellie visited often because there were only two houses on The Hill, the Catlins' and the Dowes'.

"I think you're crazy," Sid said as they turned into the drive. "Why should you come all the way up here just to talk to Kathleen?"

"I told Jesse I would explain to her what happened," Ellie said. She pulled a piece of paper from her pocket. "And give her this note."

When Sid pulled the car to a stop at the front entrance, he glanced at the note then at her. "This is rough on you, isn't it?"

She shrugged, trying to make the movement casual. "I'll survive. I just want Jesse to be happy. And if Kathleen will make him happy, then that's what I want."

The silence drew out, and she could feel the intensity of his stare. After a moment she said shortly, "Okay, it's not what I want. And it hurts like crazy. But I have to do it anyway."

Drawing in a bracing breath, she stepped from the car and walked to the front entrance. The wide carved door opened almost as soon as she rang the bell.

"Hello, Jodie," she said to the maid. She tried to act casual, as though visiting Kathleen were an everyday thing. "How's your mama? Is her hip getting better? We miss her in the choir."

"Well, hi, Ella Mae," the tall, thin woman answered in surprise. "Mama's doing a lot better." She fell silent, looking at Ellie expectantly.

Ellie shifted her weight to the other foot then inhaled and said in a rush, "Is Miss Kathleen in?"

"She's here, Ella Mae," Jodie said, her face doubtful. "But I don't know if she's receiving guests."

"You mean you don't think she'll see me." Ellie smiled ruefully. "Well, tell her I'm here anyway."

The maid shrugged and let her walk into the entry hall, then walked toward the rear of the house. Ellie watched her go in uneasy silence, then she glanced around the wide hall. It was bigger than the Cooper's living room. The parquet floor shone like a layer of golden brown glass. Although she wasn't an expert, Ellie knew that every table, every painting was the best that could be had.

She had been to the Dowes' years ago for one of Kathleen's elaborate birthday parties. That was the year Kathleen's mother had decided to give the underprivileged kids of Bitter a treat. But charity had its limits, and they had been carted from town in one of the estate's work trucks rather than the Cadillac. After an extensive tour of the house, during which they were warned by a servant not to leave grubby fingerprints on anything, they filed into a room to receive cake and ice cream and to pay homage to the reigning princess, Kathleen.

Ellie smiled at the memory. Mrs. Dowe had never forgiven her for tripping Kathleen that day and causing the blond girl to get her new dress muddy. The older woman still referred to Ellie as "that nasty little Cooper girl."

Ellie had been standing in the hall for a good ten minutes before Kathleen finally appeared. The older girl wore white hip-hugging slacks and a short, pink top that showed her pale midriff. She walked with the assurance of a queen in her kingdom.

"Hi, Ella Mae," she said. Kathleen's smile was calculated to convey a message—that she knew she was being kind to speak to someone so far beneath her. "Jodie said you want to see me. Why don't we go into the den?"

Ellie followed her, rolling her eyes at the unsubtle sway of the blonde's hips. Since there was no one there to admire her technique, Ellie figured Kathleen must spend times like these getting in some practice.

In the large, wood-paneled den, Ellie didn't waste any time with pleasantries. "Have you heard about Jessie?" she asked bluntly.

Kathleen carefully avoided her eyes. "Yes, Daddy told me all about it. It's terrible, just terrible."

"He asked me to give you this." Ellie's voice was brusque and unsympathetic as she handed the other girl the note.

Kathleen scanned the note quickly then shoved it into a pocket that didn't look like it had room for even a thin piece of paper. She avoided Ellie's eyes, biting her lip as the silence drew out.

At last, in exasperation, Ellie said, "Well? Are you going to go see him or not?"

"You know I want to see him, Ella Mae." Kathleen glanced up and Ellie saw her eyes. For once she thought the Prom Queen was actually sincere. "I *truly* do," Kathleen said emphatically, then her pale blue eyes sought the dial of the delicate gold watch adorning her equally delicate wrist. "It must be just *awful* for him. My heart positively hurts when I think of what he's going through."

"Come on, Kathleen," Ellie said, deciding the other girl's sincerity, though real, wasn't worth much. "Are you going to see him or not?"

The older girl frowned in displeasure. Ellie knew Kathleen didn't approve of such a direct manner of speaking. She had always liked the ruffles and lace veils that went with polite conversation.

After a moment Kathleen sighed. "I want to, but Daddy wouldn't let me go to the *jail*." The way Kathleen said it, it sounded like a trip to Devil's Island instead of the county jail. "I just know he wouldn't."

"You mean you haven't even asked him yet?" Ellie didn't try to hide her contempt.

"I don't have to ask." Her voice was slightly defensive. "I know he wouldn't like it."

"I don't imagine he would like you making out in the bed of Jesse's pickup, either, but that didn't seem to slow you down any," Ellie said with heavy sarcasm.

A startled gasp escaped the blonde as her hand moved to her throat. "Who told you?" she asked weakly.

"Don't get your drawers in a tangle." Ellie eyed her in contempt. "No one else knows."

Kathleen swiveled sharply and moved to stare out the window. "You sound so condemning," she said, twisting nervously at a ring on her little finger. "You don't know how it is. When I'm with Jesse, it's...oh, it's just the most exciting thing I've ever known."

Ellie stiffened. She didn't want to hear this. She didn't want to hear the unconscious sensuality in Kathleen's voice when she spoke of Jesse.

"He doesn't treat me like I'll break," the other girl continued. "When he touches me—"

"That's enough," Ellie rasped harshly.

Sweet heaven, she thought, how much torture could she take? She inhaled slowly. Then the corner of her mouth curled up in a smile of self-admission. Who did she think she was kidding? Ellie knew if it was for Jesse she could take anything anyone could dish out.

"This is getting us nowhere," Ellie said, her voice stiff but calm now. "Will you at least go to the courtroom tomorrow? This is all some crazy mistake, and as soon as Mr. Catlin can talk, he'll tell everybody so. But in the meantime, it sure would mean a lot to Jesse if you could manage to be there for the arraignment."

Once again the blonde glanced nervously at her watch. "I just don't see how I can, Ella Mae. But ... but you tell him I'm thinking of him."

"Well, that ought to make everything all right," Ellie said with open contempt. "Since I'm obviously keeping you from something *really* important, I'll go now."

At the door of the study, Ellie glanced back over her shoulder and stared at the other girl for a moment, then she said softly, "You know, I used to envy you, Kathleen." Then she walked out.

Ellie paused in the hall, trying to calm her temper. She had never imagined the confrontation would be so frustrating. But no matter how much she wished it, she couldn't make Kathleen go to see Jesse.

Brushing her hair off her forehead in exasperation, Ellie walked toward the front door. But when she reached out to open it, it swung wide to meet her hand, and old Mrs. Catlin, Palmer's grandmother, walked in.

Her posture, her expression, everything about the matriarch of the Catlin family seemed designed for repression. Her short hair was blue-white and every curl was in exactly the right place, as though they too were intimidated by the old lady. Her face was smooth and pink between the lines, her makeup carefully applied.

"Ella Mae Cooper?" the old lady said, squinting at her. "Is that you?"

"Yes, ma'am, Mrs. Catlin. I was just visiting with Kathleen." She paused uncomfortably then added, "I'm real sorry about your son. I hope he gets better soon."

"He will or he won't," she said gruffly. "It's in God's hands now. Straighten your dress, girl. Your petticoat's showing." She walked past Ellie without another word and headed toward the den.

"Yes, ma'am," Ellie said, pulling at her skirt. Suddenly she felt a strange prickle of warning and, glancing up, she saw Palmer standing in the doorway grinning at her, his enjoyment obvious.

"So, Ellie honey," he drawled. "Didn't I tell you Jesse wouldn't last long with Kathy?"

Ellie wished she were a man so she could wipe the silly smirk off Palmer's face. But without the muscle, she could only use words. "Doesn't it make you feel small, Palmer, to know that the only way you could win was for Jesse to be taken out of the picture?"

He laughed. "Not at all. I knew that before long he would screw up. In fact, I was counting on it. Being Jesse, he had to make waves sooner or later—and Kathy doesn't like waves." He glanced beyond her to the doorway of the den where Kathleen was welcoming his grandmother. "We're alike, Kathy and I. We're selfish people," he said quietly. Then he shrugged as though he had long become used to the fact. "You can see we belong together."

Ellie didn't think she would ever come to like Palmer. But just for a second, for a lightning moment out of time, she felt a kind of kinship. For the first time she realized that, as much as he was capable of loving, Palmer loved Kathleen. And, like Ellie, he was aching to have his love returned.

Without speaking, Ellie passed him and walked toward the car. There was nothing more she could do here. She wouldn't tell Jesse what she had seen and heard.

As she approached Sid's car she saw that it was empty. Glancing around hurriedly, she found Sid with the top half of his thin body being swallowed by the open hood of old Mrs. Palmer's Lincoln Continental.

"What are you doing?" she asked as she reached him.

Raising up slightly, he pursed his lips and said, " 'There's a rattle, boy. See if you can find it.' " His imitation of Palmer's grandmother was perfect, and Ellie laughed.

"I'm glad to know that she scares you as much as she does me," she said. "She reminds me of Queen Victoria. I always expect her to use the royal 'We.'"

He grinned, reaching up to pull down the hood. "I've done all I can. If it still rattles she'll have to get Palmer to fix it."

"As if," Ellie said, giving an indelicate snort, "he'd agree to take a chance on getting his hands dirty. He could never do it. He gets confused at a self-service filling station."

They turned and walked together toward Sid's car. Ellie could feel Sid's gaze on her, sense his concern. She couldn't handle his sympathy, it would be too much on top of everything else.

As soon as they pulled out of the drive, he said gently, "Was it bad?"

She nodded. How could she explain what it was like to hear Kathleen describe how it felt when Jesse made love to her? She was still fighting to overcome the burning pain in her head and in her chest.

After a moment she inhaled raggedly. "She won't go to see him."

"Did you think she would?"

"She's supposed to care about him," she said in angry bewilderment. "If she really tried she could influence her father. He might be able to help Jesse. But she won't even try. She won't even talk to him."

Sidney stared straight ahead. Several miles went by before he spoke. "You might as well face it, Ellie. You and me, we're all Jesse's got."

Chapter Six

Ellie arrived at the courthouse early the next day. She felt very small sitting alone on the wooden bench. Anxiety had kept her awake another night and she felt strangely disoriented as she watched people file into the courtroom.

Luke and his group of friends were among the first to arrive. They didn't look at all subdued by the austere atmosphere, but punched each other playfully, laughing and talking in loud whispers.

Palmer and Mr. Dowe entered together, both wearing similar tailor-made suits and similar looks of untouchable dignity, as though they weren't pleased to be in such a common place but were well aware of their duty.

But Palmer and Mr. Dowe and Luke were a minority in the courtroom, and as the room slowly filled, Ellie found her confidence growing. The usual observers also came in—people like Mr. Arnold and Mr. Sisk, dedicated checker opponents who had both been retired from the army for twenty years; and Mrs. Annie Wells, a widow who always sat on the back bench with her crochet work.

These people weren't bad, Ellie thought as she watched. She knew these people. She had lived with them most of her life. They wouldn't let Jesse get hurt.

Mr. Marshall sat at the front of the room, shuffling through papers. A door to the side of the room opened and Jesse was ushered in. When Ellie saw he was wearing his plaid shirt, she figured it was his lawyer's attempt to make Jesse look respectable. But nothing could hide the kinetic energy he exuded and nothing could dampen the blatant sensuality of his hard, muscular body.

Jesse's appearance had an immediate effect on the people in the courtroom. In the various faces around the room there were many different reactions—sympathy and animosity, envy and lust, depending on whether the viewer were male or female, honest or corrupt.

Even though he must have been aware of the charged atmosphere, Jesse held himself proud. As she studied the lines of his strong face, Ellie felt she had never loved him more than she did at that moment. Her feelings for him had always been tinged with hidden desperation; she had wanted him to love her so badly. But now her need was shelved and her love strengthened. All she wanted was for Jesse to be free. She wouldn't ask God for more.

His unshakable confidence began to soothe her ragged nerves. But after a moment she wondered if her nerves hadn't been the only thing holding her together. As her muscles relaxed for the first time in two days she began to feel a peculiar weakness overcome her.

Hold on, she told herself, trying to clear her thoughts. She had to be alert for what came next.

The uniformed policeman had left Jesse at a table with Mr. Marshall and moved to stand to one side. Jesse's head was bent to the smaller man's, and they were talking in whispers that couldn't be heard above the buzz of voices coming from the spectators.

Ellie watched them intently. Mr. Marshall had said there was a chance that Jesse wouldn't even go to trial, she thought, hope welling up inside her. *It's all a terrible mistake,* she assured herself. *In a little while everything will be like it was before.*

Ellie glanced up when Grannie Jean and Grampa walked in and sat beside her. She smiled at Sidney's parents across the room. Jesse wasn't alone. He had friends.

When the judge entered, she pulled herself up straighter and listened in confused silence to the proceedings. Ellie didn't know what she expected. It was all happening so fast, so unemotionally. She had thought that when you were dealing with a man's freedom you should spend a little time on it. But she was wrong.

Although she couldn't understand the legal talk—from the district attorney and from Jesse's lawyer—all too soon there were words that were impossible to misunderstand, and suddenly the courtroom swam before her eyes.

Bound over for trial.

It couldn't be. She couldn't have heard right. Ellie stood awkwardly, her thoughts chaotic, her blood singing crazily in her ears. She had to talk to Jesse and find out what they were going to do now. Faces swam before her eyes. They seemed to be talking, but she couldn't hear what they said. Judge Edwards's words were echoing too loudly in her head.

"Jesse." Ellie thought she had whispered the word, but the people around her were turning to stare.

"Jesse!" She moved toward the end of the bench, tripping over feet and purses in her haste.

She saw him stiffen, then he turned around, anxiously searching the courtroom, his strong face lined with concern. He took a step toward her, but immediately the policeman who had accompanied him into the courtroom grasped his arm. Ellie began to move up the center aisle, her feet leaden. When someone tried to pull her back, she shook loose. She had to keep going. She had to get to Jesse.

The pounding of the judge's gavel echoed in her head, matching the pounding of her blood. He was calling for order, calling for the defendant to be removed, calling for the disruptive spectator of his court to be restrained.

"Jesse!" she screamed for the last time as they led him from the courtroom. His name was still on her lips when the door closed behind him.

She swiveled frantically, staring at all the faces surrounding her. Curious faces, amused faces, concerned faces. Someone had to stop this. Couldn't they see that? It was wrong. Desperately wrong.

Then Grampa was there beside her, leading her from the courtroom. He pulled her to a bench outside the room, soothing her with words she didn't understand. No one could help. Not the lawyer whose job it was. Not Grannie or Grampa who loved her and cared for Jesse.

"I want to see Jesse, Grampa," she whispered, her voice tight. "I've got to see him."

The old man shook his head sadly. "You can't do that, sweetheart. They're not through in there. The judge has to set Jesse's bail as soon as things calm down. And they won't let you back in the courtroom."

She shook her head in frantic protest. "Why is this happening? I don't understand. He didn't *do* anything."

"I know, sweetheart, I know," he soothed. "It's not fair. But you've got to make up your mind that fair or not, it's happening. Accept that and go on from there."

She raised a trembling hand to her forehead. Grampa was right. She had to accept that it was happening and find some way to stop it. If only she could think straight, maybe she could find some way out.

He squeezed her hands tightly between his. "Mrs. Russell wants you to come over to her house so you can lay down for a while. Maybe by the time you get some rest, Jesse will be out of here."

"Mrs. Russell? Oh, Grampa," she said in weary dismay. "She always wants to tell me about her last gallbladder operation."

"She's a good Christian woman and she wants to help," he said in reproval. Then he smiled. "You just pretend like you're sleeping and she won't bother you. Your grannie and me want to stay up here in case we can help, but we don't want you to be alone." He kissed her forehead. "Will you do this for me, Ellie girl?"

Ellie sighed. She might as well go. She couldn't do anything here. Maybe if she were by herself, she could think of something. "Okay, I'll go over there." She twisted on the wooden bench to face him. "But you'll let me know if anything happens?"

"Of course we will."

Three hours later Ellie was lying on a bed in Mrs. Russell's spare room. She had done Grannie Jean's friend an injustice. After insisting that Ellie eat a Spam sandwich, the older woman had left her alone to think.

The yellowed shade at the window was pulled all the way down, leaving the room full of dusky shadows. Ellie stared at a sharply defined sliver of trespassing sunlight, trying to find answers in the slow-moving galaxies of dust motes. She didn't hear the door open.

"Ella Mae?"

She sat up eagerly. "Grampa? What happened? Why did it take so long?"

He sat on the bed beside her. "It took your grannie a while to arrange for bail," he said. "She had to pull in a few favors, but he's out now."

Her thoughts were frantic as she stood up. "He's out? I've got to go find him."

"That's why I came to tell you," he said, squeezing her hand. "Jeanie still has some business to take care of, but Jesse's been out for almost an hour now and I knew he'd come lookin' for you."

She leaned down to give her grandfather a distracted kiss then rushed out of the room. If Jesse had been out that long, he may have already been by the house. But she would find him, wherever he was. She had to find him.

Jesse flipped his cigarette out the window of the pickup, his eyes on The Hill ahead, his mind on Ellie. Where was she? he wondered edgily. She had looked so scared in the courtroom. Jesse had never spent much time regretting the fact that he was always in trouble. But when he had seen Ellie's pale face and heard the terror in her voice when she called his name, regret struck deep.

He shifted uncomfortably in the seat. He would get things straightened out with Kathleen, then he would go back to Ellie's house and wait. He would take care of her like he had always done.

Five minutes later he rang the doorbell at Kathleen's front door.

"Hi, Jesse," Jodie said nervously. She had opened the door only a crack, just enough to allow her to talk. "What can I do for you?"

"You know what I want, Jodie," he said, his voice calm and low. "I'm here to see Kathleen."

"Now, Jesse," she said, glancing over her shoulder. "You know I can't let you in. With the trouble you're in, Mr. Dowe won't let you anywhere near Miss Kathleen."

He was silent for a moment, then he nodded. "And Miss Kathleen? What does she have to say about it?"

Again she glanced over her shoulder. "Miss Kathleen's a good girl. She wouldn't go against her daddy."

Someone was listening. Apparently Mr. Dowe was checking to see that Jodie followed orders. Lowering his voice, Jesse said, "Tell her to meet me at the shack at the back of Otis Bates's property. At ten tonight. Tell her it's important and I'm depending on her. Will you do that, Jodie?"

She looked doubtful, but she nodded. Then loudly, she said, "Now you just better leave, Jesse."

As he drove down from The Hill, Jesse felt heavy. Although he knew he had cause, he had taken care never to give in to self-pity. He had always fought against railing at the fates that orchestrated his life. But suddenly everything seemed to be closing in on him.

Why should things work out for him now? he wondered grimly. When had they ever worked out for him? Even before his mother had left town there had been the constant arguments between his parents, sudden disappearances on his mother's part. Then when she left for good his father had started to drink. Their roles had instantly reversed. The man Jesse had always counted on for support and love suddenly couldn't manage to dress himself without help.

When Kathleen had started taking an interest in him, Jesse thought things were finally going his way. Kathleen pulled him up in the eyes of the world. And more importantly, in his own eyes.

She had to come, he thought, his hands clenched on the wheel. She had to.

Ellie felt a stitch tear at her side, but she didn't slow her quick pace. She had wasted so much time already. It had been two hours since Jesse was released. Someone had told her they saw his blue pickup at the Pixie. But he wasn't there, and she had thrown away precious time.

When she finally turned the corner on to her own street, Ellie went weak with relief. The blue pickup was parked in front of Jesse's house. Breaking into a run, she swung into the untidy front yard and jumped up the three sagging steps to the porch.

She started banging on the door. "Jesse!" she shouted. "Jesse, it's Ellie."

She had started to knock again when the door swung open. Mr. Perkins squinted against the sun, swaying a little. "Ella Mae. What's wrong?"

"Hello, Mr. Perkins," she said, her voice breathless. "Where's Jesse?"

"Jesse?"

"Mr. Perkins," she said anxiously. "Isn't Jesse here? His truck is in the driveway."

He peered over her shoulder at the pickup, but he still looked as though he were having trouble taking in what she was saying.

"I . . . I think I saw him." He rubbed his unshaven chin, his hand trembling, his eyes confused. "But I thought it was a dream." He glanced up, his expression pleading. "Wasn't it a dream, Ella Mae? Was Jesse here?"

"You don't even know if he was here?" she asked incredulously. She couldn't believe it. He was too drunk to know if his son needed him or not.

Mr. Perkins must have recognized something in her eyes. It was the first time she had ever shown him anything other than respect, and he withdrew visibly from her.

"I'm . . . I'm not feeling well," he mumbled. "I'd better go back to bed. I can't think when I don't feel good. Jesse always tells me to . . ."

His voice faded as he walked toward his bedroom, leaving the front door open. Ellie reached out to pull it closed. She didn't have time to feel sympathy for Mr. Perkins. She had to find Jesse.

She looked to the west, toward Mr. Bates's property, toward the cabin. That's where he would be. There was no place else for him to go.

Inhaling deeply, Ellie started walking.

When she finally reached the cabin, she was exhausted. Rushing forward, she threw open the door, her heart pounding against her chest in expectancy. She found the cabin empty. Jesse wasn't there.

Disappointment swept over her, swamping her, draining her of her last remaining strength. She almost sat down on the floor and cried in anger and frustration. Instead she leaned against the wall in the far corner of the room, trying to decide what to do next.

After a couple of minutes of disjointed thought, she knew it was no use. She was too tired to think logically. Wearily she slid to the floor.

Leaning her head against some empty crates, she remembered how they had used the same crates to house the injured animals Ellie had adopted over the years. Jesse had always helped her take care of them until they were well. One year there had been a coyote....

Ellie shook her head, fighting to keep her eyes from closing. She tried to remember what she had just been thinking about. But she couldn't recall the memory, and against her will, her eyes closed at last.

Chapter Seven

Ellie came abruptly awake. Her pulse thudded in her ears as her eyes darted around the darkness in confusion. Then she leaned her head back against the wall, squeezing her eyes shut in disappointment.

She remembered now. It was night and she was in the cabin. And Jesse hadn't shown up.

What was she going to do? Ellie wondered wearily. Where could he be? She had been positive he would come to the cabin. It was all her own fault, she told herself heatedly. She should have gone straight to the house as soon as she left the courtroom. She should never have let Grampa talk her into going to Mrs. Russell's house to rest. Now there was no telling where he was.

As she sat there, her mind began to work at last and it suddenly occurred to her that Jesse was probably home in bed. She felt like a fool, sitting on the floor, waiting for him when he was probably sleeping.

Ellie inhaled slowly, deciding she had better get home herself. By the coolness and the depth of the darkness, she could tell it was very late. Ellie had never stayed out after dark without letting her grandparents know where she was. Grannie Jean was going to kill her for sure, she thought, sighing in resignation.

Placing her hands on the floor, she began to push herself up, recognizing the soreness in her limbs without paying much attention to it. Then suddenly a noise broke the silence and she froze.

It was only a small sound, a minute rearranging of the silence. But it was enough to tell her that she wasn't alone in the cabin. If she hadn't been so worried she would have known it before; the very air around her seemed to give off signals.

It couldn't be Jesse, she thought, biting her lip nervously. He would have found her and awakened her.

She held her breath. Ellie wasn't often frightened and she didn't like the feeling now. She knew that no one ever came to the cabin except Jesse and herself. But it wasn't impossible that some drifter had managed to find his way to their secret place.

Memories of childhood stories came to her, stories told only in the dark, stories about madmen with chainsaws, monsters wielding meat hooks. But before the visions had a chance to get out of hand, she heard someone muttering and closed her eyes in relief. It was Jesse. He must have been too preoccupied to see her in the dark corner where she rested.

She opened her mouth to let him know she was there, then suddenly she closed it again. Something wasn't right. His voice sounded strange, almost wild, and not as strong as usual. It sounded hesitant as though he were talking with marbles in his mouth.

Peering around the crates into the darkness, her eyes widened in surprise and concern as she at last interpreted the peculiar quality of his voice. Jesse was drunk!

It simply wasn't possible, she thought in bewilderment. Jesse didn't drink. Because of his father, he had never given in to what he considered a terrible weakness. He even refused to drink an occasional beer when Sid had one. At least that was how it had always been, she thought ruefully. Right now he was very definitely drunk.

Oh, Jesse, she thought in despair. *What are you doing to yourself?*

She drooped wearily. Now when he needed her more than he ever had, Ellie knew she couldn't help him. She couldn't even let him know she was in the cabin. She knew Jesse as well as she knew herself. He wouldn't want anyone, even Ellie, to see him in this condition. He would be so ashamed.

Settling back against the wall, she made up her mind to stay hidden and wait until he was asleep or until he left. Her muscles ached to stretch out, but she ignored them, curling up with her arms linked around her knees.

He began moving restlessly around the small room, and Ellie started when he stumbled against something. She waited until his swearing stopped, then relaxed again against the wall. Jesse was talking to himself in a low, harsh whisper, and although she tried not to hear, eventually his words began to get through to her.

"She didn't come," he whispered savagely to the darkness. "She didn't even send a message. Why did I think she would? Why should she want to see me?" He paused and she thought maybe he was drinking again. "Where in the hell is Ellie? Why didn't she wait for me? No Kathleen...no Ellie...*no damn Jesse.*"

He kicked something and the noise made Ellie flinch. She wanted so badly to go to him, but she realized that would only make it worse. It would sicken him to know that anyone knew of his weakness.

"Damn you, Kathleen," he said harshly. "Why didn't you come?"

Ellie put her hands over her ears. She didn't want to hear. She didn't want to know that he had told Kathleen about their secret place. That he had allowed the Prom Queen to cause him to go against his principles and get drunk.

Tears ran unheeded down her cheeks, angry tears, hurt tears. Her fingers couldn't block out the sound and she cried silently as she heard him say over and over, "No damn good. I'm no damn good."

The pain in her chest was unbearable. After what seemed like years, there was total silence in the cabin, and Ellie decided he must have fallen asleep on the cot. She felt drained of all energy, as though she had been through a war in the short time she had been listening to him, but she forced herself to move. She had to leave while she could.

Moonlight filtered through the dirty, burlap-covered window. As she tiptoed across the room, she saw Jesse lying on the bare cot. She held her breath, but he didn't stir and she decided he was sleeping.

Just as she reached the door, Ellie heard a sound she couldn't believe she was hearing and swung around. It was an ugly sound, a raw sound. Jesse was crying.

Ellie felt like screaming. This couldn't be happening. A nothing, a nobody like Kathleen shouldn't be allowed to cause such pain in someone as strong, as good as Jesse.

Ellie couldn't stop herself as she walked across the room toward him. The sound of his anguish was too much to bear. When she sat on the edge of the cot and leaned over him, touching his face, he twitched as though he knew something were not quite right. Then, as though the motion was automatic, he moved into her, sliding her body down so that he could hold her, feel her warmth.

She caught her breath, then slipped her arms around his waist, hugging him tightly, willing the strength of her body to be transferred to his and give him ease from the pain.

They lay there for long, intense moments, merely holding each other. Then Ellie began to stroke him, his face, his back, petting him like an injured animal. Compassion and love blended in an overwhelming combination.

When his mouth found hers, she kissed him eagerly. Then something wonderful happened. Ellie had kissed Jesse dozens of times in the past, but this time was different. His tongue entered her mouth, prying her lips apart, searching for something she didn't understand. She opened her mouth to ask him, but he slipped his tongue between her teeth, delving deeply.

Strange sensations were taking over. When Luke had tried to kiss her like this, she had found the experience unpleasant, disgusting even. But this was Jesse. His every touch brought a new, urgent kind of pleasure. Her body felt flushed, like it had when she had been down with the flu. The heat felt electrified, and an unexplainable dampness came between her legs.

Hesitantly she met his tongue with her own, more than willing to explore this new sensation. Her movement drew a deep sighing groan from the back of his throat that startled her. Then his hand came up to capture one high, round breast. She had often dreamed of Jesse touching her like this, but she had never imagined that one touch would cause explosions of sensations to shake through her body. She whimpered and moved against his fingers.

He reacted to her encouragement wildly. His breathing was erratic and his fingers were awkward with haste as he began to unbutton her blouse. She felt his hand at her back, fumbling for the hook to her bra. When her breasts were free, he sighed heavily and pressed his face against their softness.

All Grannie Jean's careful warnings were forgotten as Ellie felt the heat of his mouth against her skin and the moist roughness of his tongue on one taut nipple then the other.

Tentatively, she raised her hands and began to unbutton the plaid shirt with trembling fingers. He would stop her if it was not what he wanted, she decided. But she needed to feel his bare flesh against hers.

When she moved forward and pressed her breasts into his hard chest, he gave a wild, frantic cry and grasped her buttocks with both hands. He pulled her hips against his, thrusting against her, letting her feel the iron strength of his need.

It never entered her head to try to stop him when he unzipped her jeans. She watched in fascination as he pushed the cotton panties down and began to kiss her stomach. Then his hand slid between her thighs and touched her, finding the heat and the dampness.

He groaned and the sound was pleasure, as though she had done something wonderful. Her breath caught in her throat as she felt the electric response of her own body to his hands.

Things were happening inside her that she couldn't control. A strange, aching heat was pulsing between her thighs. Her breasts felt larger, fuller and were sensitive even to his slightest touch.

With shaking hands, she helped him remove her jeans, then his own. And at last they were naked. As their bodies pressed together instinctively, she knew this was what she had been waiting for. Her mind hadn't known, but her body had. To have Jesse touching her, kissing her, needing her was the reason she was a woman.

When he reached down to spread her thighs and moved his body over hers, Ellie felt a moment of fear, but only a moment. If she could have stopped him, she wouldn't. Because she couldn't stop herself.

She felt the hard heat and pushed up awkwardly to meet him. There was pain, a sharp burning pain as she felt something inside her tear. But the pain didn't matter. She was *glad*. She almost sobbed with the intensity of the emotion. She was glad because this was Jesse. Because he needed *her*. Not Kathleen. He needed Ella Mae Cooper—red hair, freckles and all.

When he felt her stiffen slightly and heard the small cry that escaped her, Jesse tried to ease the hurt with soft kisses and soothing, loving words. And he succeeded. He not only eased the pain, he rekindled the fire.

He rocked on her gently until she was used to the feel of him inside her, until she began to dig her fingers into his back for more. Then he began to love her with slow, provocative strokes that drove her out of her mind.

When the agony of her need had wiped away all memory of pain, the rhythm increased. She met each hard stroke hungrily and soon felt an all-consuming tension grip her body.

She wanted ... she wanted something. She had to have it. Her frantic fingers and anxious lips begged for it. Her body screamed for it.

Then without warning an earthquake rocked her. It felt as though her body were composed of a thousand tightly coiled springs that were suddenly and magically released, jolting the earth around her. So deep was she in the incredible pleasure, she barely heard the triumphant cry that came from Jesse.

Then warmth flooded her and they sagged together, their bodies jerking spasmodically, their breathing harsh. The lethargy spreading through her reached her brain, and for a moment Ellie thought she lost consciousness. But she didn't let go of him. She felt nothing could make her leave his side again. There was a wholeness about her that was totally unfamiliar. Knowledge had been given to her, and the beauty of it, the wonder of it, held her in thrall.

The love she had always felt for this man swelled inside her, growing past all boundaries, taking root in every part of her. Every inch of her belonged to Jesse. She lifted her hand to stroke his cheek, tears starting in her eyes as she was overwhelmed by the strength of her love for him.

Then with crystal clarity, Jesse whispered, "Kathleen ... Oh God, Kathleen."

The world stopped. With agonizing slowness, a silent scream formed in her head and Ellie felt the word rip through her as a white-hot bullet tearing at her insides, killing her.

Sweet heaven, no, she thought wildly as she began to shake. She couldn't stop. For a long time she lay there struggling for each harsh breath. She expected tears; she *wanted* tears. But they didn't come. No relief was allowed her.

And as Ellie lay beside Jesse on the bare cot, a part of her died, the child part, the open part. She had heard people talk about part of them dying, but she hadn't known that the dying was painful. That you could feel the part being ripped away.

Then inevitably a dreadful numbness began to spread through her, and she felt the pain being sucked from her. She had never felt so strange. It was as though she had been removed from the earth and flung into alien territory, alone. Alone with millions of cold dead worlds. There was no one to save her, no one to care, no one to warm her.

Her eyes were glazed, her movements stiff as she slowly rose from the cot. She was strangely objective—as though she were someplace else viewing her actions—as she used her panties to wipe her thighs then slipped them into the pocket of her jeans. Moving automatically, she finished dressing. Jesse hadn't stirred, and she didn't look back as she walked out of the cabin.

Outside the world was the same. The same stars shone; the same warm dry wind brushed her face. The trees and rocks were all familiar, but changed. She didn't belong anymore. She wasn't a part of this. She wasn't real anymore.

She walked off the hill, stumbling often, feeling her separateness but not caring. She crossed the empty field at the bottom of the hill and entered Bitter, strolling along the deserted streets as though she were walking to the A&P for Grannie Jean and as though everything were still the same and she weren't merely an empty shell.

When she reached the street, Ellie saw people in front of Jesse's house. She saw them, but the meaning of them didn't reach her. She would have walked right into the policemen that were gathered there if Sidney hadn't caught her before she got too close, grabbing her arm to pull her behind a hedge.

She looked up at him in curiosity. Moonlight left darker shadows on his already dark face.

"Ellie," he said in exasperation. "Where the hell have you been?"

She frowned. The anxiety in his voice finally penetrated her false calm. "What is it?" she said, her brain still sluggish. "What's happened?"

"Mr. Catlin is dead," he said bluntly then nodded toward the police. "They're waiting for Jesse... or you. His bail has been revoked."

Feeling returned to Ellie in a painful rush, rocking her back, sucking the breath from her lungs. *Jesse!* They were waiting to take him away again.

"Where's Jesse?" Sid's voice interrupted her chaotic thoughts.

"He's at the cabin." She pulled her arm free. "I've got to tell him what's happened."

"I'll come, too." As they turned away, he touched her arm and whispered, "Wait."

She followed his gaze back to Jesse's house. A big silver car had pulled up to join the police cars.

Kathleen's father stepped from the Cadillac and waited silently for Chief Sharpe to reach him. Then the two men started to talk.

Ellie looked at Sid with wide eyes. He was frowning, his eyes puzzled and angry. He glanced down at her, then grabbing her arm, he began to run.

By the time they reached the cabin, Sid was half pulling, half carrying her. He threw open the door, and, while he was waiting for his eyes to adjust, Ellie ran to the cot.

"Jesse!" She grabbed his bare shoulders to shake him. "Jesse, you've got to get up. They're looking for you. *Jesse*," she repeated desperately.

"Judas priest," Sid said in exasperation when he reached the bed. "He's buck naked. And stinking drunk to boot. Help me get his clothes on him."

It wasn't easy because Jesse was deadweight, but they at last managed to get his pants and shoes on him. When Ellie began pushing one arm through his shirt sleeve, Jesse began to rouse.

"Ellie?" he said in confusion. "Was it a dream? Was it all a dream?"

"Yes," she said, her voice sad. "It was just a dream." She pushed his hair back on his forehead. "Come on, help me with this shirt. You've got to get out of here."

Awkwardly he shoved his other arm into the sleeve then glanced up. "Sid? What are you doing here?"

"That's what we're trying to tell you, you damn fool. The police are trying to find you. Old man Catlin died. They're going to haul you in again."

Jesse shuddered. "I don't know if I can take that again," he said grimly. "I'm not used to being closed in. It eats at you."

"Then get up off your ass and let's get out of here," Sid said. "I've got a cousin in El Paso who'll hide us."

Jesse still wasn't himself because he didn't even question Sid; he merely nodded.

"I'm going, too."

Ellie's words fell into silence, then both their heads swiveled slowly toward her in surprise as though they had forgotten she was there.

"You're crazy if you think—"

"No way in hell—"

They both spoke at once, then stopped when she shook her head stubbornly. "You can't stop me. If you don't take me with you, I'll hitchhike to El Paso."

"Don't be stupid," Jesse said, anger strengthening his speech.

"Look," Sid said. "We can argue about this later. Right now we need to get Jesse out of Bitter."

Ellie hesitated and then nodded. Sid was right; they had to get Jesse out. Anything else could wait. The three of them stood and moved to the door.

When they walked out into the moonlight, Chief Sharpe and two of his men came striding into the clearing.

Ellie felt Jesse go tense beside her, and as though it was her own, she felt his apprehension, his anxiety so acute it was close to panic. And she also felt the exact moment he gave up, the moment he became resigned to being taken in again.

"No, Jesse," she whispered in desperation. *"No."*

He didn't move until two policemen stepped forward each to take one of his arms.

"Leave him alone!" she screamed, slapping at them futilely with open hands. "No! *Let him go*."

With no more than an irritated glance, one of the policemen shoved Ellie aside and she tripped, falling to her knees. Jesse jerked an arm free to help her, but it was no use. They wouldn't let him go back.

Sidney helped her to her feet, and together they watched the four figures disappear into the trees.

Think, Ellie, think, she ordered silently. This couldn't be the end of it. There had to be someone in the town who knew that Jesse was innocent. Someone had to know that he wasn't with Mr. Catlin at the time of the attack.

Using every bit of strength she could pull together, she willed her body to stop shaking; she forced strength into her limbs, into her mind, and set her jaw in determination.

Someone in Bitter knew the truth. And Ellie had just decided she was going to find that person, no matter what she had to do.

Chapter Eight

Ellie slowed her steps. By the yellow light of the street lamp she could see the square, brick First National Bank building ahead. And beside the bank was the concrete lot where Luke's group gathered on Saturday nights. They parked their souped-up cars in a circle and each radio, tuned to the same Odessa station, would blare rock music into the circle.

Ellie had never joined them there, but she knew that a lot of alcohol was passed around. On Sunday mornings empty beer bottles and occasionally a half-spent pint of bourbon stood in a circle on the parking lot until after church, when the bank grounds-keeper came to dispose of them.

She could see the cars now. Leaning against the hoods were kids she knew from school. Most of them she had known since she was eight but none intimately. They were too wild to be friends with a girl as closely guarded as Ellie. They were girls who wore their skirts too short and their makeup too heavy and boys who were continually looking for excitement and went to school only because they were forced to do so.

Luke was the oldest of these. He was the same age as Jesse, but he had never moved into the adult world as Jesse had. He preferred hanging around with younger troublemakers because his age made him the leader.

As she walked closer, Ellie picked him out. He was leaning against the door of his red Mustang. She almost turned around and ran, but she knew she couldn't. Taking deep breaths to slow her heartbeat, she approached him.

Laughter and loud voices died away as she neared, until there was only the sound of the music. It was Golden Oldie weekend at the radio station, and Buddy Holly's "Peggy Sue" blared in her ears as she walked. She didn't look at the others but kept her eyes on Luke.

When she was standing directly before him, she could see Luke's confusion. He didn't know whether to make fun of her or show his pleasure at seeing her.

She gazed up at him, then without speaking, she reached up and removed the half-smoked cigarette from his lips, put it to her own and pulled deeply on it. "Hi, Luke," she said after a tense moment.

"What are you up to, Ellie?" he asked, suspicion making his voice hard.

She shrugged, a carefully casual movement. "Nothing. That's the problem." She leaned against the Mustang beside him, her shoulders hunched forward in discontent. "I'm bored stiff, Luke. With Jesse in jail there's nothing to do."

He stared down at her for a moment, then suddenly he laughed in triumph. Throwing his arm around her, he said, "I've got a bottle in the car. That ought to liven things up for you."

As though his laughter had released them from a spell, the others started talking and laughing again, pretending they didn't notice when Luke Owens pulled Ella Mae Cooper into the back seat of his car.

Jesse leaned against the concrete wall, staring through the bars into the darkness outside. His face was thinner than normal, his eyes immeasurably older. The front of the jail faced the courthouse across the street. But back where Jesse was, there was nothing, nothing but miles of Texas.

He glanced back over his shoulder into the cell. His gaze passed over the two bunks, the toilet and the sink without seeing them. Every day the cell grew smaller until it seemed to be closing in on him.

He had memorized all the graffiti on the walls but had added none of his own. He didn't want to leave any part of himself in this place, not even a thought.

Jesse had been staring at the same graffiti and the same acre of mesquite trees for six weeks, six weeks that exceeded the bounds of reason or right. And he had no idea how much longer he would be there. Marshall kept postponing the trial date in his attempt to get a change of venue. But at this point Jesse was almost willing to take his chance in Bitter just to get it over with.

In the time he had been in the county jail Jesse had changed. It wasn't merely the endless hours alone. It was the thoughts inside his head that were driving him crazy, keeping him awake nights.

He had had too much time to think over everything in his life, and he was deeply dissatisfied by what he had found. He kept looking for a pattern, for a reason to explain why he felt so restless, so out of place in Bitter. He wanted desperately to know why he didn't fit in. But he had found no answers, merely more questions.

Only one thing had become vividly clear. Jesse knew now that he had never loved Kathleen Dowe. He had discovered the truth even before her father had come to see him to tell him that Kathleen was engaged to Palmer, even before he found out that it was through Kathleen that the police had found him at the cabin.

He inhaled slowly. Memories of that night were confused. He couldn't figure out the sequence of events or even which were real and which belonged to dreams. Had Kathleen let him make love to her then immediately betrayed him? Or had it all been an illusion born in a bottle?

He shook his head in confusion. It had seemed so real. He could still feel the warmth of her in his arms. God, he could still remember the scent of her.

Dream or reality? he wondered cynically. He couldn't say, but it made no difference. He realized now that he had been so desperate to have Kathleen as his girl because he thought that would make him somebody. That knowledge only added to his dissatisfaction.

He moved restlessly across the cell, pacing a familiar path, driven by his thoughts. It had been almost a week since Ellie had been to see him. He was worried about her. She was usually there every day, cheering him up, keeping him sane with her smiles and her blunt opinions of Bitter's officials. They both pretended that his being locked up was nothing, that it was a stupid inconvenience. But Jesse knew it was weighing Ellie down. He could see the changes in her.

He frowned suddenly. Lately there had been more. In the past couple of weeks, although she tried to hide it, Ellie had been different. She seemed nervous and constantly avoided looking him in the eye.

Everything was falling apart. It was so damn frustrating. He had to get out of here, Jesse thought fiercely. He was slowly dying inside. Although he tried to act natural when Sid or Grannie Jean came to see him, at times he thought he would go crazy if he didn't get out soon. He had taken his freedom for granted. He had always had the whole of the Texas countryside to roam around in. Being limited to such a small space was eating away at him.

His hatred of the town and his role in it had grown until it was ready to burst inside him. Slamming his fist against the wall, he asked himself how long it could possibly last. Was he destined to spend the rest of his life working in the gravel pits? Would he have to stand by and watch his father slowly kill himself?

He knew the answer to both questions was yes. Jesse would never be anything as long as he was trapped in other people's opinions of him.

For a long while, Jesse sat on the bare bunk and stared at his hands clenched in his lap. When he heard a key in the cell door, he turned his head slowly.

Frank Newbody was there, swinging open the door. Jesse didn't speak; he just stared at the older man in silent frustration.

"You can go, Jesse."

"What are you talking about?" Jesse said sharply. "Go where?"

"Out. You're free."

Jesse didn't move. Every muscle tightened. He couldn't think rationally. This was some kind of trick to make his stay more unbearable. One more thing to cause him pain. They were trying to drive him crazy.

"New evidence has turned up," the man continued as casually as if he were discussing the weather. "All charges have been dismissed."

"Evidence?" Jesse managed to say at last. "What kind of evidence?"

Newbody shrugged. "Don't know. They don't tell me anything. All's I know is the chief don't like being wrong. My orders were to wait until late and let you go as quietly as possible."

Jesse inhaled slowly. It was like a message, he thought. All the pain of living in this town, all the doubts that had hounded him during the past six weeks had been leading to this. From now on he would be his only judge. Jesse himself would decide when he was somebody.

He stood, knowing now what he had to do. Now, tonight before he had a chance to change his mind, Jesse had to leave Bitter.

Ellie lay on her back in bed, staring silently at the ceiling. She tried to keep her mind off the tightness in her chest and in her throat. But she couldn't ignore how tired, how terribly weary she was. She had felt the same for two long weeks. Ever since...

But she didn't want to think of that. She had to keep her mind on the fact that Jesse was going to be free. It was all worth it—all the pain, all the humiliation—if Jesse could only be free.

She rubbed her eyes. They burned and so did her throat. Suddenly Ellie held herself stiff. She could have sworn she heard her name being called. Then it came again... from the window. "Jesse!"

She jumped from the bed and ran to the window, pushing open the screen so she could climb through.

As soon as Ellie stood before him in her thin cotton nightgown, Jesse caught his breath sharply. She had lost weight, weight she couldn't afford to lose, and her gray eyes overpowered her small face. Suddenly she was in his arms and he could feel her trembling. Guilt weighed heavily on him, tightening his throat. Worry had done this to her.

"God, Ellie," he whispered harshly against her brow. "You look terrible. I'm sorry. I'm so sorry."

"Hush," she said, her fingers clutching at him. "It's not your fault. I picked up some kind of bug. Honest, Jesse," she murmured. "I'm fine. Now that you're out, I'm fine."

She moved her face against his chest. "Oh, Jesse. I thought I would go crazy. But it's over now. Everything will be like it was before."

"Ellie."

His voice was soft and gentle, but there was something there that she didn't want to hear. Stubbornly she closed her mind and her heart against it and tightened her arms around his waist.

"Tomorrow," she said urgently. "Tomorrow we'll go up to the cabin and . . . and go swimming. We—"

"Ellie!" he said, grasping her shoulders. "Listen to me, Peanut." When she stared up at him with wide, frightened eyes, he said, "I'm leaving, Ellie."

He felt the shudder run through her as she hid her face against him. This was the worst. All he had been through couldn't measure up to what he was feeling now. He felt her pain, her fear and wanted to change his mind.

Then she looked up and smiled sadly. "I knew you would," she whispered. "I knew that sooner or later you would leave. I was just hoping it wouldn't be for a while."

He stepped away from her, running his fingers through his hair. "I hate leaving you, but I have to." He smiled grimly. "Besides, I haven't done you much good lately."

"Don't say that!" She clutched his arm with both her hands. "Don't ever say that. You've . . . you've given me so much. You'll never know. If you've got to leave, then do it. But don't ever say I'll be happier without you.''

He pulled her back against him, feeling a strange, overwhelming emotion grip him. Forcing her chin up, he stared down at her. ''You've made my life here bearable. I don't know what I would have done without you. But . . .''

''But you don't belong in Bitter,'' she said, her voice wistful.

''I don't know, Ellie,'' he said, shaking his head. ''I don't know if the town is out of step or I am. I only know there's a world out there besides Bitter. Other towns, other people.'' He sighed roughly. ''I want to see it all. I want to see tall buildings and giant trees on the side of the highway—anything except belly-up armadillos. I want to know what a New York minute feels like. I want to see if the people in California are really crazy.'' He clenched his fists against her back. ''I want to see people who don't know that I'm that no-good Perkins boy,'' he finished grimly. ''I've got to leave Bitter. I've got to stop just existing and start living.''

She nodded against his chest. ''Yes,'' she whispered. ''You've got to leave.''

Tilting her head back, she smiled tremulously. ''Don't worry about your daddy. Grannie Jean and I will look out for him and see that he eats regularly and that he doesn't smoke in bed.''

''I'll send money,'' he said, his brow creasing in thought. ''As often as I can. And when I get settled, I'll send for him. He needs to get out of Bitter, too.''

She nodded, her face pale and ghostly in the moonlight. It hurt Jesse to think of leaving her. "Look, Ellie," he said anxiously. "We'll see each other again. Just as soon as I've made some money...as soon as I'm somebody. And...and in the meantime, we can write."

"Yes, we'll write," she whispered. Although the pain was killing her, she knew she had to let him go now, but her fingers were numb from holding on so tightly. She let her hands slide to her side and took a step back.

For a long time he stared at her in silence as though he were memorizing her features, then he turned away.

"Goodbye, Ellie," he said softly.

She didn't move until she could no longer see him. Then she reached up to wipe the tears from her cheeks.

"See you, Jesse," she whispered to the empty darkness.

Chapter Nine

November, 1985

Jesse Perkins eased his foot onto the brake to reduce the speed of the rented car. Flexing his shoulders inside the suede jacket, he tried to ease the cramped muscles. He wasn't used to inactivity, a fact made obvious by his broad shoulders and powerful neck.

After a few more miles, he glanced down at the gold watch that stood out brightly on his tanned wrist. He had made good time, but the drive had still been a long one. A plane chartered in Odessa would have made the trip easier, but Jesse had wanted his approach to Bitter to be a gradual one.

His dark gaze swept over the countryside with avid interest. In California, autumn had barely existed, while on the East Coast it had been a flashy panorama. He had forgotten how soft the colors of fall were in Texas. The leaves had turned to a color that was almost pastel, blending with one another in the distance like a faded patchwork quilt.

But it was not for the autumn scenery that he had taken the slow route. Over the years, Jesse had formed the habit of dissecting his emotions. Now he wanted to analyze his reaction to entering his hometown for the first time in eleven years.

So far he was satisfied. None of the old tension, the old pain had surfaced. There was not a trace of the trapped anxiety that he used to feel. He was pleased to find he was no longer susceptible.

Relaxing in the seat, he surveyed the area. At some time in the past, the county had widened and resurfaced the highway for it was now four lanes. He wondered wryly if it was for people coming in or people trying to get out.

The thought made him smile slightly. If he could still think of the town so harshly, some of the old hostility must remain. But maybe hostility wasn't the word, he thought. Perhaps cynicism was a better description. It wasn't any more agreeable than hostility, but agreeable or not, a man didn't get to Jesse's age and position without gaining a little cynicism along the way.

Passing a burgeoning housing subdivision, he checked it out with rising interest. The rows of boxy, modern houses weren't the first sign of growth Jesse had seen. He had known that eleven years would inevitably bring some changes, but somehow he had expected those changes to be minor.

When he passed the city limits sign, he did a double take, whistling under his breath. Apparently the town of Bitter, Texas, population under two thousand when he had left, now boasted more than twelve thousand people.

He laughed softly. It was time for a little honesty, he thought wryly. Even though he had told himself there would be changes, deep down he had expected Bitter to be the same as he had left it, a kind of Brigadoon that existed only when he was there to see it.

Maybe he had wanted it to be the same. Wasn't he just a little disappointed to find that Bitter had prospered? Could it be that there was still a little of the old antagonism left, he wondered wryly. Or was it simply that he wanted to step back into the past and show all the good citizens that Jesse Perkins was somebody after all?

As he drove he found even more surprises. On the left he passed a modern shopping center, containing among other things a discount store and, unbelievably, a French restaurant. By the side of the highway there were several fast-food places. But the biggest surprise came when he spotted a couple of motels, real motels with swimming pools and restaurants attached, not four little stucco cabins with a burned out Vacant sign in front. Bitter had come up in the world.

Closer to town, he saw several unfamiliar companies, companies that didn't have the Catlin or Dowe name attached. They appeared to be thriving and must have brought in a number of new people.

When at last he passed through the town proper, Jesse saw that this had changed the least. The courthouse was the same, as was the jail. He slowed to look at the place that had changed his life, then surveyed the rest of the square. The other buildings had been given a face-lift at some point, but underneath they were still Dowe's Variety Store and the Curl Up and Dye Beauty Salon.

There were many new faces on the streets, faces that should have looked out of place but didn't. The feel of the town was different. These people belonged. It was Jesse who was the intruder now.

Searching carefully, he began to pick out familiar places. Fred's barbecue place was still where it had always been beside the Fina station. He smiled. Fred made the best ribs in the world. There were times in the past eleven years that he would have given his soul to have a slab of those ribs.

It was a major disappointment to find that the Pixie Drive-in was gone and a car wash had taken its place. It probably hadn't been able to compete with the more efficient, fast-food places.

He turned a corner and spotted the old Wolters place where he, Ellie and Sid had spent one hilarious Halloween. They had scared the pants off Palmer Catlin, he recalled, chuckling at the memory. He stared at the house, filled with nostalgia. Someone had renovated it, turning the old Victorian home into a picturesque tea room.

His brow creased as he thought of Ellie. The memory of her was strong now that he was actually in Bitter. Against his will, he thought of the last time he had seen her. Even now he couldn't forget the way she had clung to him. Through the years the pain in her eyes had stayed with him, haunting him when he least expected it.

As he promised, Jesse had written to her, frequently in the first year. Then when she hadn't answered even once, his correspondence had dwindled to a yearly birthday card, all of which went unacknowledged. After a while he had stopped altogether.

He couldn't make himself believe that Ellie had simply ignored his letters. The only sense he could make of it was that she and the Coopers must have moved away from Bitter shortly after he left town.

When his father had joined him in L.A., Jesse had questioned him closely for news of Ellie and Sid. It was frustrating for them both to realize that his father had been too drunk when he was in Bitter to know what was happening.

The memories began to sweep over him now. He smiled when he remembered how besotted he had been over Kathleen Dowe. Lord, he had been so foolish back then. The only thing she had ever given him was one night, the night he had gotten drunk and made love to her.

He couldn't remember a single, solid detail of that night; he didn't even know if it was truth or a figment of his imagination. All he could remember was the way he had felt. He had felt so overwhelmingly loved, so filled with warmth and security. He hadn't been able to shake the memory. Even when Kathleen had refused to see him in jail and when she had become engaged to Palmer, it had stayed with him. All his relationships through the years had been measured against that feeling and had been found lacking.

Now that he was in town he wasn't sure if he would look Kathleen up. Too many things had changed. He didn't think a meeting with her would accomplish anything. *But then you never know,* he thought. If there was a chance, he would probably take it. It was time he exorcised that particular ghost and got on with his life.

Ostensibly Jesse was returning to Bitter for business purposes. He was checking into prospective sites for a new plant, but he knew very well he could have sent someone else. He had always meant to come back to Bitter, had always wanted to find out about Ellie and perhaps to clear up his feelings about the past. But he was here at this particular time because of three letters.

He glanced down at the briefcase on the seat beside him. The letters inside the leather case were identical, each stating that his arrest eleven years earlier had not been a mistake. They claimed that Jesse had been set up, and that Mr. Catlin had not been killed by a transient as had been the official opinion.

It all sounded a little far-fetched and was most likely the work of a crackpot, but he had decided no harm could come from checking them out. Jesse wasn't out for revenge, but if the truth happened to come to light while he was in town, so much the better.

As he approached the south side of town, the buildings thinned out. Rubbing his stiff neck, Jesse decided to go back to one of the motels and get a room. He had a lot of work to do and had only allowed himself a week in which to do it.

As he turned the car, a woman caught his eye and he slowed to watch her. She was a small woman but shapely with a narrow waist and firm, round breasts, both features shown to advantage by an electric pink sundress that left her tanned shoulders bare. Her hair was the warm color of sun-ripened peaches, not red exactly, but then not blond either. It fell around her shoulders in a cascade of vibrant curls. Jesse raised one eyebrow speculatively. This was definitely not a woman who intended to be ignored.

She was locking the door of a small, square building. The large, wooden letters on the side identified it as the Carrol County Veterinary Clinic. Jesse felt a spark of excitement quicken his pulse. There was something strikingly familiar about her, about the way she carried herself, the way she tossed back her hair.

Switching off the engine, he got out of the car and began to walk toward her. As he drew nearer, he knew his instincts hadn't failed him.

Suddenly, as though she had heard his footsteps, she swung around. Even after all the years, he found he could still read her emotions in her beautiful, ex-

pressive face. In rapid succession, it registered confusion, astonishment, pain, then finally joy as she
whispered, *"Jesse,"* and walked into his arms.

Chapter Ten

I can't believe it," Ellie said, her voice husky with astonishment. "I simply can't believe it."

She pulled back from Jesse, her eyes searching his face intently. It was Jesse's face, but it had changed. It had filled out and maturity had softened the harsh lines. But the sensuality was the same. It was still there in his lower lip, in the intensity of his dark eyes.

She shook her head, her eyes wide in disbelief. "After all these years, you simply walk up to me on the street. If that isn't just like you," she said, the words tumbling out. "What are you doing here? How long can you stay? How did you find me?" She paused to catch her breath. "It's incredible. Simply incredible."

Her breathless monologue made him laugh. "I'm a little shocked myself," he said, his eyes never leaving her face as though the sight of it intrigued him. "I can't believe it's really you, Peanut."

Her eyes closed helplessly as the nickname took her back eleven years. Fighting the memories, she drew in a deep breath then opened her eyes. A slow smile of genuine welcome curved her lips. "Welcome back, Jesse."

He hugged her again. "God, Ellie, it's so good to see you. I don't know what I expected to find here, but it certainly wasn't you." He shook his head as he stared at her in amazement. "And all grown up, too."

"This is not exactly what I expected when I got up this morning, either," she said, laughing.

He glanced at the building behind her. "What are you doing here? Is one of your strays sick?"

She smiled. "Something like that," she said, then she glanced around and shook her head. "What are we doing standing here? Come back to the house and we can get caught up on everything." Her gaze caught the silver Lincoln. "I suppose you still know the way."

He laughed. "Everything's changed so much, I doubt I could find it. But don't worry, I'll stick close."

As she drove, Ellie checked her rearview mirror often. She still couldn't believe it. Jesse was back. Delirious excitement raced in her veins. She felt exhilarated, breathless. All these emotions she acknowledged. She carefully shut her mind to the others.

Now that she was out of his presence, Ellie found herself becoming a little apprehensive. What would they talk about? she wondered, biting her lip. It had been eleven years. Would they still have anything in common?

He looked very prosperous, she thought, frowning. How could he still be the same Jesse when he had lived in a different world for so many years? After they had caught up on the years, what then? Would they suddenly be two people who were too embarrassed to admit that they were actually strangers?

She shook her head. Of course Jesse wasn't the same. But then neither was Ellie. That wouldn't keep her from being pleased to see an old friend. Yes, she could manage that easily enough.

When she reached the house, Ellie stood beside her small red sports car and waited for him to get out of his car. When he joined her, he stood for a moment looking at the house next door. His gaze lingered on the neat green shutters, the newly mowed lawn.

"The Albertsons bought the place about five years ago," she said quietly. "They're good neighbors."

He didn't answer right away but stared as though seeing the house as it had been in the past when he and his father lived there. For a moment it was as though the old Jesse stood beside her. She could almost feel the conflicting emotions he was feeling. Then he turned back to her and smiled. Instantly, the past dissolved.

Glancing around the yard in curiosity, he said, "Didn't there used to be a bed of zinnias over there? And...and four o'clocks there?"

She glanced at him in surprise. "I can't believe you remember that. Yes, Grannie Jean used to keep flowers everywhere. I'm afraid I don't have the time or patience that she had."

"Had?" he asked frowning. "I'm sorry, Ellie. I didn't know."

"There's no reason why you should," she said reasonably. "It was almost three years ago. She broke her hip then developed pneumonia in the hospital." She smiled, but it didn't reach her eyes. "She was strong-willed to the very last."

"And your grandfather?"

"About eight years ago," she said, her voice gruff. "A stroke."

She shook her head, then a movement across the street caught her eye and she waved. "Hello, Mr. Crump," she shouted. "Look who's back. It's Jesse Perkins."

She glanced at Jesse. "Say hello to him," she whispered. "He doesn't get much company anymore."

"Do I have to?" he asked. "He always used to just frown and nod at me. It made me feel like a dog he strongly suspected had made a puddle on his best rug."

"Oh, come on, Jesse," she urged, laughing. "It'll tickle him."

"Hello, Mr. Crump," he yelled, waving. Then as the old man frowned and nodded, Jesse added in an undertone, "He looks tickled all right. Are you sure all this excitement is good for him?"

Laughing, she unlocked the front door. He followed her inside and paused, inspecting the living room as closely as he had the yard. His gaze lingered long on the changes. There was a pale green carpet instead of bare wood floors. Most of the old, heavy furniture was gone, and in its place stood brightly colored, modern furniture.

She waited for a comment, but he was silent as he slowly examined the room.

She shifted her weight to the other foot. "I've changed a few things."

"Yes, I see," he said quietly. After a moment he glanced back at her. "I like it," he said firmly. "But it feels a little strange. Mr. Cooper's chair should be over there by the door—and the whatnot shelf should be there." He nodded toward the corner.

"It's been eleven years. Things change," she said, unaware of the abruptness of her tone. She drew in a slow, bracing breath. "Well, don't let's just stand here. Sit down. Tell me about yourself."

Tossing her purse on a chair, she moved across the room. When she turned, she was a little disconcerted to find him directly behind her. He smiled as he sat down beside her on the couch. "You've got to go first." He glanced at the slender hands that rested in her lap. "You never married?"

She shook her head vigorously. "Who has time for marriage? How about you?"

"I've been kind of busy myself," he said, smiling ruefully. "I wish I could say I came close, but the truth is I can't seem to find what I'm looking for." He shrugged. "A severe flaw in my personality, no doubt," he murmured, his voice dry. Then he glanced up. "Now, tell me what you were doing at that clinic. You were locking the door, so you either work there or you've become a . . . *cat* burglar."

She laughed as she shook her head. "Oh, that's awful. Is that what you've learned out in the big, wide world—to make lousy jokes?"

"That's a big part of it, I'm afraid," he said, laughing wryly. "Now tell me."

"If you had looked closer at the outside wall of the clinic you would have seen E. M. Cooper, DVM. I'm a veterinarian, which shouldn't surprise you considering how often you helped me tend the wounded." She shifted in her seat, finding a more comfortable spot. "You know how determined Grampa was that I go to college. I just wish he had been there to see me graduate." She glanced up, her gaze becoming distant and clouded. "He died in my sophomore year. And Grannie Jean missed him every day of the rest of her life." She leaned forward, her expression earnest. "You know, Jesse, on the surface she appeared to be the stronger of the two. We never realized how much she depended on him."

When she found him staring at her, studying her face, Ellie pulled herself up sharply. "Okay, now it's your turn," she said. "Tell me every single thing that happened to you after you left here."

"Everything?" he repeated, raising one dark brow.

"Everything. Starting from the night you left." She ran her gray eyes over him assessingly. "You look very...uptown. So some pretty exciting things must have happened after that night."

"A long time after," he said ruefully. "I left without having any real idea of where I was going and not enough money to get there. I started heading west, and when I reached El Paso, I stayed for a while with Sid's cousin, working at odd jobs to make enough money to move on." He leaned back, his eyes directed toward the past. "After El Paso, I kept moving west. It took a while, but I eventually landed in Los Angeles. And then..." He paused, and surprisingly he seemed a little uncomfortable. "Well anyway, I began making enough money to allow me to go to school nights."

"Wait a minute," she objected. "Back up. You're leaving something out." She grinned. "What did you do in Los Angeles—sell your body or something?"

"You little witch," he said, laughing. "You always enjoyed making me squirm."

Ellie didn't take the bait, and when she continued to stare at him with wide-eyed expectancy, he moved his hands in exasperation and said, "Okay, okay. I took bit parts in movies. Now are you satisfied?"

"Movies!" she exclaimed in excitement. "I can't believe it. Why didn't I ever hear about it? We do get movies here in Bitter."

"I'm afraid they're not the kind of movies you would see in Bitter," he said hesitantly.

"Oh, Jesse," she said, holding back her laughter with difficulty. "Were you a porn star?"

"No, I wasn't," he said sharply, then reluctantly he smiled. "You would love that, wouldn't you?" He shook his head. "They weren't pornographic, but there was a certain amount of nudity. They called them art films. I personally didn't remove so much as a shoe," he said emphatically then smiled and shook his head. "It was all a little crazy. This wild Italian director got it in his head that I was symbolic of something—brooding youth, I think he said—and for the next three years I would pop up, a little like Alfred Hitchcock, in all Mario's films."

"How fun," she said enthusiastically. "And I think he was right. Back then you were the absolute epitome of brooding youth, some might even have called it sulking youth."

He stared at her laughing face. "How long has it been since I boxed your jaw?" he asked softly.

"Not long enough," she said. "Now tell me the rest."

"When I finished college—I was lucky and managed to do it in only three years—I had a degree in business. I had the knowledge, but I didn't have a job. The director had found a new symbol by that time, and I was tired of that kind of thing anyway. I was ready to use what I had learned, but so were a thousand other graduates. From the acting jobs, I had saved a little money and managed to borrow some more, and I bought a hot-dog stand on the beach."

He glanced at her doubtfully. "That doesn't sound very exciting, I know. But I made good money at that stand. In about six months, I bought another one. The next part is weird, but then California is a little weird. I had the girls who worked at the stands wear cowboy hats, boots and spangled miniskirts and called them Texas hot dogs, and suddenly—almost overnight—the places were jam-packed.'' He shrugged. ''It took a lot of work and even more fancy footwork, but eventually I had a chain and was advertising on television and radio. I had had them three years when a conglomerate bought me out.''

Leaning back, he smiled. ''And that's how it started. I'm what people call an entrepreneur.'' He grinned and looked ten years younger. ''Which means that one day I'm rich and the next day I can't afford one of those Texas hot dogs. Actually it's not that bad,'' he admitted. ''I've made some investments that should keep me solid. I was wildcatting for a while and bought into the company. And then I have a couple of moderately successful supper clubs. The plant site I'm looking for right now is very speculative. The company is on the rocks and it's anybody's guess as to whether I can turn it around.''

She whistled under her breath, her raised brows showing her appreciation. ''I'm impressed. It's an honest-to-gosh Horatio Alger story. *Luck and Pluck* or maybe *Ragged Dick*,'' she said impudently, laughing at his disgusted expression. ''And now you've come back to the hometown that scorned you. Are you here to thumb your nose at the Golden Circle?''

He shook his head. ''Nothing so dramatic, I'm afraid. It's mainly business. I'm honestly checking out building sites.'' When she looked skeptical, he gave a short laugh and said, "Okay, maybe a part of me wanted to say 'Hey, look at me.' But it doesn't matter, does it? Everything has changed. It's obvious by the growth I've seen that the Catlins and the Dowes no longer run the county."

She rubbed her chin with the knuckle of her forefinger, her eyes thoughtful. "It's changed," she said. "But there are some things that never change. Our erstwhile social leaders are still active. It's just that now the Dowes and the Catlins make up only a small part of the Golden Circle. But they're still rich, and they're still snobs." She grinned. "And I thumb my nose at them every day. It really galls people who have snubbed me all my life when they have to call me about a sick animal." She paused, giving him a significant look. "You see, I happen to be the only vet within one hundred miles."

"That's wonderful," he said, laughing in appreciation when she batted her eyelashes at him guilelessly.

The whole time she had been speaking Jesse had studied her mobile face. His eyes were pensive when he asked quietly, "Why did you stay, Ellie? Surely a larger town would have offered you more."

"At first it was for Grannie Jean," she said slowly. "Then the town began to grow and the new people didn't care who I had been, only who I am now."

Jesse stared at her in thoughtful silence. Her explanation sounded reasonable, he assured himself. So why did he sense that she was suddenly shutting him out? There was something about her carefully casual expression that told him not to press her, but he couldn't prevent his curiosity from growing immeasurably.

"Tell me about your father," she said, breaking the silence. "I remember the day he got the bus ticket you sent him." She smiled at the memory. "He was so excited about going to join you at last . . . but still reluctant to leave, I think. Although deep down he knew things couldn't continue as they were, he was afraid of starting over again. But he wanted to change for you . . . and in the end, for himself."

He nodded slowly. "He was sick for a year after he joined me in Los Angeles. Alcohol had been a part of his life for a long time. It took its toll. And when he was actually, finally sober, he couldn't remember even half of the years that had gone before." He studied her face. "He couldn't remember whether you were still in Bitter or not."

"I was here," she said, her voice bright. "So he's all right now. I'm glad."

"I'm used to his sobriety now, but I don't think I'll ever forget what it was like," he said, his voice rough. Then he made a visible effort to shake off the melancholy memory. "He's remarried, you know. Betty makes sure he faithfully attends his AA meetings. She keeps him in line, but in such a loving way that he doesn't mind."

"That's fantastic," she said, her genuine pleasure reflected in her face. "Do you like her?"

"Very much. She's good for him."

"It's hard to believe that he finally gave up on your mother," Ellie said softly. "It's sad in a way. He loved her so much."

"He loves Betty," he said. "But in a different, less obsessive way. The other was a terrible, destructive kind of love."

Ellie glanced away. Unwittingly, he had struck a nerve and she had to struggle to regain her composure. "So you're in town on business?" she asked after a moment, keeping her voice casual as she stared down at her hands.

"Partly," he said. "I do need to check out a plant site, but there were...other things." He paused, giving her a crooked smile before he continued. "I've been receiving anonymous letters."

She raised her eyebrows. "That certainly sounds intriguing."

"A fifties melodrama is what it sounds like—small screen, black-and-white film, and all," he said dryly. "About two months ago I got a letter. No name, no return address. It was typed and merely stated that my arrest eleven years ago hadn't been a mistake. I was set up."

She whistled. "And do you believe it?"

"I don't know. It wasn't like I received a blinding revelation or anything. I just ignored it, but then two more letters came, both exactly like the first." He shrugged. "I had been planning to come back anyway so I figured now was a good time."

She stared at him thoughtfully. "So you're going to see that justice is done at last?"

He grimaced. "That's a little strong. I'm not really intent on finding out about an old crime, but something might turn up while I'm here." He caught her eyes and held them, studying her peculiar expression. "You wouldn't happen to know who wrote those letters, would you?"

"I couldn't say positively," she said reluctantly. "But I might have an idea."

"The plot thickens," he said, grinning. "I didn't really expect to find the writer. But I figured it wouldn't hurt to check with the police and see what the records show about the Catlin case."

He paused, waiting for her to tell him, wondering about the strange tone she had used, as though she were getting into a subject she would rather avoid.

He gave her a bewildered smile. "You are going to tell me, aren't you?"

Supporting her chin with her thumb, she glanced at him from the corner of her eye. "Several months ago there was an article about you in the Bitter *Tribune*—it has a new owner now. It was one of those local-boy-makes-good things." She smiled. "So you see, I knew a little of what you've told me about yourself." She hesitated then said, "Kathleen saw the article, too."

"You think she sent the letters?" he asked in surprise.

"I can't be positive," she said, shrugging her shoulders. "I'm just guessing. But Kathleen and Palmer—you knew they were married?" When he nodded she continued. "I'm afraid their marriage has been a little shaky for quite a while." She raised her hands, palms up. "It just seems likely by the way she went on and on about that article that she could have written to you simply to stir things up."

He made an exasperated sound. "You mean just because Kathleen got bored, she decided to call in an old flame? What a crock."

Ellie examined his face carefully. "She's still very beautiful, you know."

He stared down at her, his dark eyes growing even darker. "She couldn't be as beautiful as you are." Leaning closer, he gently touched her cheek with his forefinger. "But I always knew you would be."

He continued to stare, and as the silence drew out, the atmosphere in the room became electric with tension—vibrant, sensual tension. There was an awareness between them that had never been there in the past. It made her catch her breath in shock. Ellie was dazed by how quickly it had appeared. She hadn't expected that type of thing, not now, not with Jesse. It made her feel uneasy, vulnerable. But she didn't have the strength to look away from his eyes. She almost felt she was drowning in the darkness of them.

As though they were being controlled by a force beyond them, they leaned toward each other. When their lips were on the verge of touching, Ellie drew in a sharp breath and pulled back hastily.

Immediately she knew she had overreacted and wondered if her embarrassment showed on her face. Neither spoke for a moment, and suddenly she felt like laughing. Her behavior was bordering on the ridiculous.

"So," he said at last, his voice unsteady. "Tell me about Bitter and all the changes I've seen."

She glanced up, relieved to have been given a subject for safe conversation. When her eyes met his, she found they were dancing with amusement. After a moment of confusion, she began to laugh.

"Stop making fun of me," she demanded, reaching over to give him a soft punch on the arm. "I feel silly enough already. I keep forgetting it's you, my own, dear blood brother. Oh, remember the time—"

"How could I forget?" he said, interrupting her. "That ritual may have mingled our blood forever in the time-honored tradition, but I've still got a scar on my finger. When rain's on the way it starts throbbing like the devil."

"It's your fault," she said righteously. "You weren't specific enough. You didn't tell me how deep to cut."

"Well, if that isn't just like you," he said indignantly. "You always managed to make it my fault because I was older. I still think you wanted to practice being a vet and were bent on amputation."

Ellie couldn't stop laughing. His outrage now was nothing to what it had been then. Memories came washing over her, pulling her emotions toward yesterday. She felt Jesse's arm around her shoulders, heard his laughter and it felt so natural, so right.

He leaned his head against hers, staring at her sparkling eyes. Suddenly his lips brushed hers. "I've missed you, Ellie," he said huskily. "I didn't realize how much until now."

She couldn't find her voice, but merely stared at him, her eyes wide.

When Jesse bent to kiss her again, something went awry. The kiss was intended to be a gesture of affection toward an old friend, but somehow it became heated and incredibly, incredibly exciting. As he involuntarily moved closer, an astonished joy began to grow in him.

After the first moment of shock, Ellie reveled in the feel of his mouth on hers. This time there could be no mistake, she thought in triumph. This time he knew who he was kissing. She could feel the desire in him and it was for *her*.

But the feeling of triumph didn't last long; she didn't give it a chance. Welling up from a place deep inside her, anger gripped her, replacing every other emotion. She raised her arms, frantically pushing him away.

God! she thought as she stood and walked away, her back straight and stiff. She couldn't let him do it to her again. She refused to be drawn into the same old spell, the same old pain.

Exhaling slowly, Jesse leaned back and watched Ellie pace restlessly about the room, her face tight. The kiss had surprised him, but there was more than surprise in Ellie's expression. There was anger and, amazingly, fear.

Quietly and with great deliberation, he said, "Why didn't you answer my letters?"

It was a second before his question penetrated Ellie's chaotic thoughts. When it did, the room spun around her, her blood pounding in her ears. *He had written*. He had actually written.

Sweet heaven, she thought in despair. All those years. All those long, lonely years.

Raising a trembling hand to her brow, she tried to make sense of it. How could it have happened. But instinctively she knew there was only one answer. Grannie Jean must have kept the letters from her. Ellie felt a deep sorrow weigh her down when she thought of the motives behind her grandmother's actions.

"I'm sorry," she said, her voice barely audible. "I didn't know you had written. Grannie Jean must have destroyed your letters before I could see them."

Jesse frowned, his expression confused, his eyes hurt. "I don't understand. Your grandmother always liked me. Why would she do something like that?"

Ellie glanced out the window, avoiding his gaze. "I don't know. She probably wanted me to stop brooding about the past and start thinking about the future." She smiled. "I was pretty lost after losing my best friend."

"But I still don't understand—" he began.

She interrupted him with a soft laugh. "Oh, whoever understood Grannie Jean?" She glanced at her watch. "I wish we could talk some more, Jesse, but I've got to get out to the Lowrey place and check on a horse."

She was shutting him out. Jesse could feel it, but he could find no explanation. This was more than just a natural hesitation between people who hadn't seen each other in a long time. It wasn't just the years that were coming between them. She was doing it deliberately. And at some time, some way, he intended to find out why.

He smiled down at her. "Okay, I'll let you run me off this time. But, Ellie," he said, catching and holding her eyes, "I'll be in town for a week—and I expect to spend most of that time with you. So don't say you weren't warned."

She laughed, but there was a wariness about her gray eyes that stayed with him as he drove away from her house. *Oh, Peanut,* he thought wearily. *What's happened to us?*

Chapter Eleven

Jesse stepped out of the shower and grabbed a towel from the chrome rack. As he dried vigorously, the muscles of his hard body were reflected in the foggy mirror of the motel room's blue-tiled bathroom. The scar on his thigh stood out vividly on his dark skin. He had acquired it while working on an oil rig in Wyoming, and seeing it always brought back memories of those days.

So much had happened in the past eleven years. Only now that he was back in Bitter did he realize just how much. When he had thought of Ellie over the years, it was always as a friend, his best friend. Distance hadn't changed that for him. He would find himself thinking at odd times that he wished he could show her this or tell her about that. But now that he had found her at last, he realized that friendship was only part of what he wanted from her.

The kiss they had shared had been a total surprise. Sparks had flown between them. Maybe he had moved too fast. But remembering the feel of her in his arms, he knew there was no way he could have stopped it from happening.

But her reaction was all wrong, he thought, frowning. The intensity of her anger had been out of proportion, and the unexpected pain he had seen in her gray eyes baffled him. At times she seemed like the friend he had left so many years before, still open and honest and loving. Then suddenly she would close up, shutting him out completely.

Inside Jesse didn't feel all that different, but he knew he wasn't the same person who had left Bitter in anger eleven years earlier. Maybe that was the problem. Time hadn't stood still for Ellie. She had grown, too. Maybe he needed to get to know her all over again.

He smiled. It wasn't a task that he dreaded. She had always been one of the most vital people he had ever known. And now maturity had brought a new, protective twist to that vitality. He looked forward to learning the workings of her mind, the intricacies of her smile.

But as much as he regretted it, Ellie was unavailable to him at the present. And there were other things that needed his attention. Such as Kathleen.

Some mystery, he thought wryly. If Ellie was right, those letters had simply been the action of a bored wife. He shook his head in wry humor. Apparently Kathleen was just as spoiled as she had always been.

He felt almost angry that it should be so. Because even if it had been a dream, the memory of that night in the cabin was still affecting him. He wondered how he would feel when he saw her again. Would the old attraction still be there? He didn't want to get caught up in Kathleen's life, but he needed to find out. He needed to get rid of the past so he could go on with the future.

He would go to see her and get the business of the letters straightened out. Maybe in the process, he would find out what had really happened that night.

Later, as Jesse drove toward The Hill, he was amazed to find the ten-mile stretch that had always been so bare was now dotted with houses and gas stations and convenience stores. It didn't even seem like the same place.

Checking the gas gauge, he pulled off the highway into one of the service stations. After telling the teenage boy to fill it up, Jesse walked inside to get a cold drink. The heat was another thing he had forgotten about Texas. Even in November, the heat at times was stifling.

He pulled a cold bottle from the cooler and stepped up to the counter to wait for the boy to finish with the gas so he could pay for his purchases.

"You're Jesse Perkins, ain't yuh?" someone said. "I heard you was back."

Glancing up, he saw an old man watching him from behind the counter. Jesse had been back in Bitter for every bit of three hours. He should have expected that the whole town would know about it by now.

Jesse's eyes narrowed in concentration as he stared at the overweight, gray-haired man. It was a moment before he could place him. Then he remembered. It was Chief Sharpe's father-in-law, Cletus Nugent.

Jesse had never liked Cletus. He could never look at the man without remembering the time he had caught him torturing an injured bird. Cletus had tried to convince Jesse he was putting the poor creature out of his misery. But Jesse had seen the older man's eyes. They couldn't hide the fact that he was sneaky, and he was mean.

Reluctantly, Jesse nodded in answer to the old man's question then glanced away, unwilling to start a conversation.

"I knew it was you. I never forget a face." He leaned back on his stool. "You look a little more high-toned than you did when you left Bitter. What'd you do—take up robbing banks?" He laughed in enjoyment of his own joke. Several minutes of coughing followed the laughter, then he said, "You back for good?"

"No," Jesse said, trying to keep the word from sounding curt as he walked over to a small magazine rack. "Just a short visit."

The older man stared with sly, narrow eyes, as though he were measuring Jesse. "You seen Ella Mae Cooper since you been here?"

Something about the tone of his voice made Jesse turn back to Cletus. It was smirking, suggestive.

When Jesse felt his stomach muscles tighten, he forced them to relax. That was something else he had forgotten about Bitter, he thought ruefully. He hadn't felt that urge to punch someone out in years.

"Yes," he said tightly. "I've seen her."

"She certainly turned into a looker, didn't she?" When Jesse didn't answer, he continued. "Yeah, she's somethin' all right. *All* her men friends think so." He chuckled. "That girl sure does stay busy."

Jesse stared down at the old man in taut silence. He wanted to take him and shove his head into the cooler. He wanted that more than anything. His fists were clenched at his side as he worked to calm himself down.

At last he could unclench his fingers, secure in the knowledge that they wouldn't automatically grab the other man by the throat. Cletus was a stupid old man, Jesse told himself. He had always been a vicious gossip, and there was no reason to think he would have changed. Anyone as beautiful and vibrant as Ellie would automatically cause comment among people like Cletus Nugent.

Everything Jesse told himself was logical, but it was still a relief to be able to pay for his purchases and get out of striking distance of the pathetic old man.

By the time he reached The Hill, Jesse was calm and could even smile at his reaction to Cletus. Discipline and control had been two of the first lessons he had learned after he had left Bitter. He had learned them out of self-defense, and he wasn't about to forget them now.

At the base of The Hill, the road that used to lead only to the Catlins and the Dowes was now the landscaped entrance to something called Dowe Acres. A large sign stood beside the road, proclaiming pleasurable, luxurious living and instant happiness for the inhabitants.

Jesse almost laughed out loud. It seemed somehow ironic that The Hill was a subdivision. As he drove on he saw that it was as luxurious as the sign claimed, each house being situated on a two-acre plot, but it was still a subdivision. And the Catlins and the Dowes now shared The Hill with fifty or sixty other families.

The Catlin house was still the same, even the landscaping immediately around the house hadn't changed. It looked strange sitting so close to other houses, but it fit in better than the Dowe house. Where the Dowe place was of a Victorian-type grandeur, the Catlin home was sprawling and modern.

A maid answered the door. Jesse didn't recognize her, but then there were so many new people it was unlikely that he would. He winced at the sound of her strident voice as she invited him to wait in the hall while she announced him to Kathleen, her attitude casual, almost careless.

Shoving his hands in his pockets, Jesse glanced around with forced interest. Palmer and Kathleen lived very well. He was walking toward a portrait of two children when he felt someone's presence.

Turning, he saw Kathleen in the doorway. She stood there for a full minute, either to adjust to the surprise or to give him an extended view of her love-liness.

Kathleen was still lovely. She was more slender than she had been eleven years earlier, her features sharper, hard even. But her sultry beauty was un-changed...and she could have been a complete stranger. He felt nothing but curiosity when he looked at her.

"Jesse," she said, her voice breathless as she walked across the hall and threw herself violently into his arms. "Oh, Jesse, Jesse. It's been so very long...too long." She leaned back to stare up at him. "I've missed you," she whispered huskily.

Carefully detaching himself, Jesse smiled. "That's nice to hear," he said. "You look great, Kathleen."

"So do you." She brushed her long hair back with one hand as she eyed his custom-made suit, the gold cuff links and watch. "Come, let's go into the den. We've got a lot of years to catch up on."

Raising one heavy brow at her eagerness, he fol-lowed her into a paneled room. Deciding against the leather couch that she indicated, he sat in a high-backed chair, hiding a smile when she took the chair opposite him, but sat right on the edge to present an image of intimacy.

In the beginning their conversation appeared to consist of simple reminiscences. But he should have remembered that nothing was simple with Kathleen. As they talked, she slowly rubbed the velvet arms of her chair in a sensual, suggestive movement. Her eye contact was designed to be provocative.

Jesse answered her questions and asked a few of his own since it seemed to be expected of him. She quickly passed over talk of Palmer and their two children and concentrated on memories of the past, all centering exclusively on herself—and on him.

"Why didn't you bring your wife, Jesse?" she asked coyly, gazing at him through her long, darkened lashes. "You *are* married, aren't you?"

"I'm afraid not," he said, his voice bland. "I envy you your family."

Her family was dismissed with a wave of her hand. "Children are wonderful, of course," she said, her voice wistful. "But like you, I've never gotten over what we had together. Our relationship was simply too intense just to fade away." She sighed effectively. "Normal conventions, ordinary morality can't enter into a deep emotional bond."

Jesse was hard-pressed to contain his laughter. Kathleen hadn't changed at all. By the signals she was sending, she obviously wanted an affair, but she couldn't manage to say the words. She had to waltz around them and over them with flowery phrases. In her self-centered mind she couldn't allow that he might not feel the same way. Ten to one, if he told her flat out that he had no interest in sleeping with her, she would call him noble.

"I wish we could talk longer, Kathleen," he said, trying to make it sound like the truth. "But I have some business to take care of." He smiled at her. "The real reason I came here was to ask about some letters I received recently."

She glanced down at her hands and smiled. "You knew immediately that I had written them, didn't you? You knew that I was anxious to clear up that dreadful mistake."

He raised one brow. "Actually, I didn't. Ellie was the one who seemed to think you might have written them."

"Ellie?" Her face hardened. "You've already seen Ella Mae?"

He nodded. "Was there some reason I shouldn't?"

"No, of course not," she said, her soft laugh sounding forced. "Considering what good friends you were, it would be strange if you hadn't looked her up. What did you think of your old playmate?"

Sensing her jealousy, he hid a smile. "I didn't come here to talk about Ellie. What makes you believe I was set up eleven years ago?"

Her expression was earnest as she moved and managed to get even closer. "I've thought a lot about this, Jesse. You know, about the way things happened. It was too convenient that you were arrested. I'm almost sure my father hired someone to rob Mr. Catlin—I don't think he intended him to be hurt, you understand," she added hastily. "Something must have gone wrong."

"And what makes you think he set me up?"

"Daddy knew how very much I loved you," she said passionately, moving to kneel on the floor before him in a very affecting pose. "He would have done just about anything to put a stop to it."

He shook his head. "I'm sorry, Kathleen. That simply doesn't gel. He could have found a dozen ways to cause trouble for me."

"You're right, of course. But I think he had had some kind of argument with Mr. Catlin," she said, eager in her attempt to convince him. "I think he wanted to get back at him. It all ties in. Mr. Catlin was hurt, and Daddy pushed the police into believing you did it."

Jesse didn't buy her story. There were too many gaping holes in it. She was trying to convince him that they had been star-crossed lovers, fighting the world. But he knew that Kathleen had never loved him. He had been desirable simply because he was taboo. And he had an idea that Kathleen's father had known that as well.

She moved closer and touched his hand, her expression shy. "I'll always regret not being stronger eleven years ago. But you see, I was scared. I'm afraid I've always been emotionally high-strung," she said softly.

Jesse was afraid that any minute she would start telling him that she had always depended on the kindness of strangers, and he didn't know if he could take that without laughing.

"You don't know how my father is when he's angry. He made so many threats." She shuddered delicately. "But I should have pulled my courage together and stood up to him." She glanced up at him through her long lashes. "If I had, I might be your wife today instead of Palmer's."

Jesse was silent, but he wondered about her statement. Yes, he had been besotted with her, but even before he was arrested, disillusionment had begun to set in. The night in the cabin might have swayed him. But now that he had seen her again, he was convinced that it had been a dream. This woman couldn't possibly give with the openness and warmth of the mysterious girl in his dream that night.

He stared down at her reflectively, wondering if he should straighten her out or simply let it go. She moved and her lips came closer. For a moment he was tempted, but only for a moment. He had begun to pull back when the door to the den swung open.

"Kathleen!" old Mrs. Catlin said, walking into the room with the help of an ebony cane. "I can't find my blue beaded bag. Why can't you do something with that girl? She's always stealing."

Kathleen jumped up. "Grandmother Catlin," she said. "You startled me. I thought you were having a nap."

Mrs. Catlin ignored her. Her narrowed eyes were focused on Jesse who had risen to his feet as she entered the room. "You're that Perkins boy," she said brusquely. "What are you doing here? If you're looking for work, you can forget it. We don't hire troublemakers." She shook her cane at him. "And you drive too fast. It isn't safe on the road with people like you around."

"Grandmother!" Kathleen said, her voice shocked. "Jesse's not here for work. He's visiting with me." She glanced up at Jesse. "He's been gone from Bitter for eleven years. Can't you tell he's very successful now?''

Jesse grinned at the old lady's contemptuous snort. Esther Catlin hadn't changed at all except for the cane. It was as though he were back in the past, still a boy from the wrong side of town. But he didn't mind. At least she was honest in her feelings.

"I apologize for my past behavior," he said humbly. "I don't drive too fast anymore."

"See that you don't," she said sharply as she turned back to Kathleen. "Search that girl's room and get my bag back." She walked to the door, mumbling as she left. "In my day, it never would have happened. The servants knew their place. We put the fear of God—"

When she was out of hearing range, Kathleen smiled apologetically. "I'm sorry, Jesse. She's impossible to live with. I'm afraid she's getting senile."

He shrugged. "She doesn't bother me. In fact, I kind of like her now." He glanced at his watch. "I'm afraid I have to leave, Kathleen."

"So soon?" she objected vehemently. "But we've got so much to catch up on." She moved nearer, just close enough so that her breasts brushed his arm. "There were so many things that I wanted to tell you." Her voice had gone soft and husky. "Couldn't you stay just a little longer?"

"Yes, Jesse, why don't you stay a while?"

They both turned to see Palmer Catlin standing in the doorway of the den. Jesse had to hide his surprise at Palmer's changed appearance. His blond hair had begun to thin, and there were bags under his eyes.

Jesse moved forward, extending his hand. "Hello, Palmer. It's been a long time."

Palmer hesitated then shook Jesse's hand. "Too long for some," he said cynically. "Not long enough for others. You look almost civilized, Jesse. Not quite so much the renegade." He grimaced. "I heard you were back."

Jesse laughed. "I had forgotten the way news travels around here. I've only been back a few hours."

Palmer walked toward his wife who was silently watching him with wary interest. "Long enough, I see," he said, leaning down to kiss Kathleen's cheek. "Hello, my darling. Your loving husband is home, seeking succor from the grueling workaday world."

"You're drunk," Kathleen said flatly. "Couldn't you come straight home for once?"

He raised one brow. "And subject you to the dullness of sobriety? Believe me, my precious, I'm much nicer, much more scintillating after I've had a snoot full."

"Do we have to go into this in front of company?" she asked peevishly.

"Don't mind me," Jesse said, keeping his voice casual. "I was just leaving anyway."

He had seen enough to realize that Ellie was right. There was a deep tension between these two people, tension that he preferred not to get caught up in. Turning, he moved toward the door.

"Wait, Jesse," Kathleen said hastily, her expression changing, becoming less resentful. "I wanted to ask you to stay for dinner."

"I can't—" he began.

"I suppose you're seeing Ellie for dinner," she said, her eyes narrowed, her voice sharp. "Well, I just hope you like company."

"What's that supposed to mean?" He was tired of innuendo and sly remarks. He wanted to get everything out in the open once and for all.

"Poor Jesse," she said, her voice fairly dripping with sweetness. "You remember Ellie the way she was before you went to jail. Sweet, innocent, little Ella Mae." She laughed. "Things change, Jesse."

"That's enough," Palmer said sharply, but his wife acted as though he hadn't spoken.

"Did you know that while you were in jail—unjustly locked up—your dear little Ellie was running with Luke Owens?" she asked.

Jesse stared at her. She was a jealous bitch. That much was obvious. Why should he believe anything she said? But something about the avidity of her pale eyes made him stay and listen.

"You wouldn't have recognized her, Jesse," she said, shaking her head with patently false sympathy. "She was drinking and smoking...and heaven knows what else. I heard she got to know the back seat of Luke's Mustang very well. No one was surprised when—"

"Stop it!" Palmer said, grabbing his wife's arm savagely. "You keep your filthy mouth off of Ellie.

You're jealous because she's got a little bit of warmth, a little bit of humanity to her.''

Kathleen turned on him. "You would know, wouldn't you?" she spat out. "In fact, you sample that warmth pretty often yourself, don't you? *Don't you?*"

Jesse leaned against the wall, unwilling to get involved, but unable to leave. He couldn't believe these two cynical people were actually discussing Ellie.

Kathleen swung away from her husband. "Do you know how many people just love to tell me how often they see your car at her house, at all hours of the night? How can you humiliate me like that? Don't you ever consider our position in this town? How can you let us become the subject of common gossip?"

Palmer was silent for a moment as he stared at his angry wife. Then when he spoke, his voice was heavy with sarcasm. "We could make a pact, my love. You give up your affairs and I'll give up mine."

Jesse didn't want to hear more of the argument. Kathleen looked like the kind of woman who was prone to throwing vases, and things looked to be building rapidly to that point. As soon as he left the den their voices became shrill, then there was a loud crash.

"I was right," he muttered, nodding politely to the maid who was listening avidly in the hall.

As he drove away from The Hill, Jesse was a mass of confusion. Palmer had not denied that he was having an affair with Ellie. But Jesse's gut feeling was that she was too straight to get mixed up with those two. And what was that business about Ellie running around with Luke eleven years ago when Jesse had been in jail?

It appeared that he had stepped into a full-blown mess and was handicapped by the fact that he was an outsider now. He knew it was none of his business, but he simply couldn't believe that Ellie would actually have an affair with Palmer Catlin.

But dammit, he thought, it *was* his business. He cared about Ellie, had always cared about her. And before he left, one way or the other, he would find out what had happened to her.

Chapter Twelve

Jessie leaned back against the square post on the corner of Ellie's porch, watching the sun go down, waiting for her to come home.

He had spent the day going over prospective sites for a new plant with Charles Sandbourn, the mayor of Bitter. Sandbourn was relatively new to the town, having lived there for only eight years. But he was sharp. Jesse had expected it to take days to get his business cleared up, but the youthful mayor had had all the labor and construction figures right at his fingertips and was even ready to give Jesse the assurance that the county would build a new road to accommodate the plant if Jesse chose Bitter as the site.

Any details that were left could be handled by Jesse's people over the phone, which meant that his business in Bitter was completed. He would leave the job of choosing a site to his experts.

He had done what he had come to do and could leave at any time. There was a club in Reno, Nevada, that he should be checking out. But Jesse wasn't in the habit of kidding himself, and he wasn't going to start now. He knew he wouldn't leave yet. Too many things had happened that he hadn't expected. All the years away hadn't changed the fact that he was still tied to Bitter.

He couldn't get the confrontation between Palmer and Kathleen out of his mind. He didn't give a damn about their marital problems, but this concerned Ellie. There were undercurrents that twisted his thoughts.

Was Ellie actually having an affair with Palmer, he wondered, frowning. The whole idea would have been impossible for the girl he used to know. But Jesse had been gone for eleven years and like Ellie had said—things change. Although he acknowledged the fact that her personal life was her own business, he felt a deep urge to shake her and say, "I didn't help raise you for this."

He had been tempted to go to the clinic to seek her out, but he wanted her undivided attention and somehow didn't think it was the right environment for a serious talk.

After leaving The Hill the night before, Jesse had stayed up late, sitting on the bed in his motel room with the scene at Kathleen's running through his mind. A vision of Ellie in Luke Owens's arms had hounded him, even in sleep. He didn't trust Kathleen, but if the part about Luke was true, Jesse had to face the fact that he himself was to blame. If he hadn't been so reckless, and so stubborn, he wouldn't have been arrested, and Ellie wouldn't have had the chance to get involved with Luke's wild crowd.

Over and over he had told himself that all that was in the past, that it didn't matter anymore. But he couldn't seem to get it out of his head. He was determined to get the truth of it from her.

Frowning, he realized that the subject could very well be a difficult one to approach. But there had always been honesty between them. No matter what else had happened, that shouldn't have changed.

Shifting his position, he wondered if maybe the business with Luke was the reason he felt a distance between them. Maybe Ellie blamed him too.

He glanced up when he heard a car pull up and watched her get out of the red sports car. Today she looked like the teenager she had been when he had left Bitter. She wore tight jeans and a loose, bright orange blouse. Her hair was in a French braid that hung down her back while peach-colored curls escaped to frame her face.

Ellie started walking toward the house, then she saw Jesse. She had recognized his car and knew he was there, but that didn't keep her heart from skipping a beat at the sight of him. Ignoring the reaction, she didn't miss a step in her stride as she moved toward him.

She smiled when she stood next to where he sat. "I certainly do get some strange looking strays nowadays," she said.

"Do you still take them in?"

She shrugged. "Once a sucker always a sucker." She unlocked the door. "Come on in and I'll feed you dinner." She paused. "Let's see—this is Tuesday. That means we have fish sticks and spinach salad."

"Those just happen to be two of my favorite things in the world," he said.

She made a face. "You must be starving to death." Walking in, she laid her purse on a small table. "Give me a couple of minutes to wash my hands, and I'll meet you in the kitchen."

In the bathroom, Ellie stared at herself in the mirror, but she saw only Jesse. It was getting easier to be around him and that pleased her. She really wanted a good relationship with him. He had been an important part of her life. She would like for them to remain friends.

As she dried her hands on a pink towel she wondered how he had reacted to seeing Kathleen. She knew she wouldn't ask him. When they had talked about the Prom Queen the day before she had detected no reaction from Jesse at all. But of course, that could mean anything. He had been good at hiding his feelings in the past, now he was even better.

In the kitchen she found him staring into the open refrigerator, surveying the contents. "The spinach is in the crisper," she said, moving to stand behind him. "You start on that while I take care of the fish."

"Kathleen thinks her father set me up on that assault charge," he said as he bent to get the spinach.

She had begun to pull out bowls and pans from the cabinet, but hesitated when he spoke, her brow creasing in thought. "Loyal little darling, isn't she?" Ellie muttered, then shrugged. "I don't know, Jesse. I guess it's a possibility. Mr. Dowe certainly wasn't hurt by John Catlin's death. There was some kind of legal agreement, and he took over almost everything that they had owned jointly. I think he had to make some kind of compensation to Catlin's family; Palmer certainly isn't hurting anyway."

She shook her head. "Somehow I never figured Mr. Dowe for the kind of man who could murder, but it certainly does sound suspicious." She turned to face him. "Does she have some kind of evidence?"

He shook his head. "I don't think so. She just seems to think he had motive and opportunity." He grinned. "She thinks he set me up because he wanted to kill the great love she had for me back then."

She raised one brow. "You sound skeptical."

"Come on, Ellie," he said, his voice derisive. "We both know that she's never loved anyone but herself. I figured that out before I ever left Bitter."

She turned back to her preparations for dinner. So Jesse had known, she thought. She was a little shocked. All these years she figured he had left still loving Kathleen.

She exhaled slowly. "Well, even without that, Mr. Dowe still had motive. Are you going to talk to him?"

He shrugged. "Probably. As long as I'm here, I might as well check it out."

His revelations regarding Kathleen seemed to release Ellie from some kind of restraint. As they prepared dinner together, they laughed and talked just as they always had. Ellie regaled him with stories of town gossip, taking pleasure in telling him that Tom Sharpe, the man who had caused Jesse so much trouble, was now the manager of a grocery store.

As they sat down in the kitchen to eat, she said, "Have you seen Sid yet?"

He paused with the fork halfway to his mouth. "Sid's here? But all my letters came back."

She frowned in confusion, then her expression cleared, and she nodded. "That's right, they moved to Dallas that fall. That's why you couldn't reach him. Sid entered SMU and took his family with him. His mother and sisters are still there, but after about five years Sid moved back, bringing a beautiful wife with him."

"You're kidding," he said, shaking his head. "So Sid's married."

"Very much married," she said with a laugh. "With three of the most adorable, rowdy kids you've ever seen."

"Sid a father; that's too much to take in." He paused thoughtfully, resting his elbows on the table. "But now that I think about it, I bet he's a great father."

"He is."

"So what's he doing in Bitter? Did he get his engineering degree like he planned?"

She nodded. "He's working for the county," she said. "He could be making ten times the money with a private firm, but he says government work is the best experience, and he might as well get it here." She grinned. "Sid is not above thumbing his nose, either."

The rest of the meal was spent remembering the crazy things the three of them had done as children. When they moved to the living room after dinner, Ellie put on a record then joined him on the couch.

As Jesse listened to the music, he leaned his head back contentedly. It was nice sitting beside her, he thought. He felt more comfortable, more at home than he did in his own apartment.

He closed his eyes and murmured lazily, "Tell me about the clinic. Do you like working with animals as much as you thought you would?"

"More," she said emphatically. "I love it. I have to confess that I lean toward the small animals. But I can't specialize here. There are too many farm and ranch animals that need me."

He opened one eye to measure visually her small frame. "I can see how you would be intimidated by anything larger than a dachshund. You're still not much bigger than a peanut."

She smiled. "That's an exaggeration, but I wish you could have seen me the first time I had to take a cow's temperature." She glared at his whoop of laughter. "It wasn't funny. The logistics of the thing were bad enough, but I was certain I would offend the hulking beast. It's not a fun thing with any animal, but cows turn around and look at you with those big Elsie eyes. It's very disconcerting. For years I found myself apologizing for the indignity before I inserted the thermometer.''

Still chuckling, he slid his arm around her waist and gave her a companionable squeeze. ''Better a cow than a bull.''

She grimaced. ''Don't talk to me about bulls. Taking the temperature is a snap compared to some of the things I have to do to bulls. I've been kicked and stepped on more times than I can count. You learn real quick to recognize the signs of imminent pain.''

As Jesse stared down into her laughing face, he felt excitement and desire streak through him. She was so damn beautiful. But it wasn't only her beauty that stirred him. She was vibrant and loving. There was a chemistry working between them that couldn't be ignored.

Without stopping to think, he lowered his head to capture her mobile lips. There was no hesitation this time. Automatically the kiss deepened. The warmth of her open mouth urged him on.

He could detect no resistence in her, not even when he pressed his body against hers and moved her until they were lying side by side on the couch. With her soft body pressing against his, he felt he was no longer in control of his actions. The taste of her drove him wild. With urgent strokes he caressed her shoulders, her arms, then sought her breasts.

Ellie caught her breath when she felt his hands slide over her breasts, long fingers manipulating her taut nipples. She couldn't think, but was carried away on a wave of sensation. All the old feelings came flooding back to her. Only now they were stronger, more powerful . . . irresistible.

This was Jesse, she thought dazedly. This was the man who had dominated her dreams for the better part of her life. This was the man she would have given her life for eleven years ago. *Eleven years ago.*

Suddenly she began pushing him away, her movements desperate. Ignoring the puzzled, hurt look on his face, she quickly slid from the couch, turning away from him to wipe her mouth with her forearm.

As strong as her desire had been, her fury with herself—and with him—was stronger. Her hands were clenched tightly as she walked to the window and stared out into the darkness that had fallen while they were eating.

Jesse watched her in silence, taking in the anger on her face. Why anger? he wondered in confusion. He had seen the same reaction the night before, but it didn't make sense. He would bet his life that she had enjoyed it as much as he had. Dammit, she had responded, he thought savagely. She had caught fire under him. Why this craziness?

"There are some things I don't understand," he said softly, his voice intense. "Things that Kathleen and Palmer said, that Cletus Nugent said . . . about you."

She glanced over her shoulder, laughing harshly. "So you've stumbled across my dubious reputation. Was that the reason for this?" She waved her hand toward the couch, an agitated movement.

He stood swiftly and walked to her, grabbing her shoulders to give her a hard shake. "You know better than that," he said tightly.

Her head dropped, and she sighed wearily. "I'm sorry. Of course I know better." Inhaling slowly, she glanced up and said, "So you've heard things about me. I assume you want an explanation."

"No," he said softly. "That wasn't what I had in mind. I guess I wanted to apologize."

"For what?" she asked in genuine bewilderment.

He ran his hand through his hair, a gesture that took her back years. Then he turned away. "I feel like it's all my fault. Kathleen said you started hanging out with Luke while I was in jail. I feel if I had been there for you, if I hadn't always been in trouble it wouldn't have happened. Dammit, you couldn't stand Luke. You must have needed someone badly."

She was silent for a while. "Yes, I needed someone," she said, her voice distant. Suddenly she shook her head in exasperation. "Why are you dragging all this up now? My God, that was eleven years ago." She stared up at him, her eyes angry. "You left. You have no right to cry about the mess you left behind."

Jesse stared at her in astonishment. There wasn't only anger in her voice and eyes; there was a deep, deep bitterness that shocked him.

She put a hand to her temple to ease the throbbing there. "I'm sorry. That was a stupid thing to say. And there is absolutely no need for you to feel guilty. None of it was your fault." She shrugged.

"Things simply happen the way they happen. My going with Luke has nothing to do with my reputation now."

Ellie could tell he didn't want to accept her evasive explanation, but apparently he wasn't going to press her. She felt her taut muscles relax in relief. She wasn't sure how much more she could take.

Her violent reaction had surprised even herself and as painful as it was, she finally admitted that the little talk she had had with herself in the bathroom had been a smoke screen. She didn't want to be friends with Jesse. Friendship would never be enough. As incredible as it seemed, after all the years, all the pain, she still loved Jesse Perkins, as surely and as deeply as ever.

And that was the real reason Ellie had never left Bitter. She had been waiting for Jesse.

Stupid, stupid, stupid! she thought angrily. After all that had happened she was still vulnerable to him. She felt like a simple-minded fool.

When she felt Jesse move to stand directly behind her, Ellie shivered violently, wrapping her arms tightly around her waist to still the tremors. Her new knowledge left her somehow exposed.

Please, she pleaded in silent desperation, *don't let him touch me.* She didn't know if she would have the strength to stop him if he tried to make love to her again.

When she felt his hand on her neck, beneath her hair, her eyelids drifted down helplessly. Her body was drawn to him irresistibly. She wanted to lean back against him and give in to the feeling. She wanted that more than she had ever wanted anything in her life.

Then suddenly, out of the blue, Grannie Jean's face appeared behind Ellie's closed lids. She winced as she saw again the silent pain she had seen so often in her grandmother's lined face.

It was enough. She stepped away from him jerkily. "I'm tired, Jesse," she said, her voice void of emotion. "I think you'd better go now."

Jesse stared blankly. Why wouldn't she let him help her, he wondered in frustration. Why did she keep pushing him away? They had had a special relationship at one time. Was it all gone? He refused to accept that. What they had had in the past and the feelings that were growing in the present were worth fighting for.

"Ellie, we've got to talk," he said urgently. "Can't we just—"

The doorbell rang, intruding, coming between them. When she opened it, Luke Owens stood on the porch.

Grim faced, Jesse stared at him. Luke still looked rough, but there was no doubt that he was a handsome man. He wore a green sport shirt with the sleeves rolled up to expose his powerful forearms. His jeans were old but clean and tight-fitting. He smiled when he saw Ellie, then his gaze went past her to Jesse, and the smile faded.

"Hello, Jesse," he said tightly. "I heard you were back in town."

Jesse nodded. "Luke," he said, stiffly acknowledging the greeting. He glanced down at Ellie, his dark eyes confused and angry. "I guess I'll be going," he said brusquely, then he turned and walked out.

"I'm sorry, Ellie," Luke said when Jesse was gone. "I didn't know he was here or I wouldn't have come."

"Don't be silly," she said wearily. "He was leaving anyway." She fought to pull her ragged nerves together. "Come on in and sit down," she said. "Tell me how the new job is going."

After five years in assembly, Luke had recently taken over as supervisor at the tool and die company. He was a hard worker and deserved the promotion.

He shrugged. "It's all right. The work is harder, but the pay is better."

"And what about that girl you met in Odessa. Did you ever call her?"

He leaned his head back. "No, I guess I forgot."

"Dammit, Luke," Ellie said in exasperation. "When are you going to get it through your head that Kathleen is married and is going to stay married? Your affair with her will lead to nothing but trouble. She'll never leave Palmer." Her voice softened as she stared at the pain in his eyes. "You'll only end up getting hurt, Luke."

"Don't you think I've told myself that?" he said harshly. "She drives me crazy." He shook his head. "But that doesn't keep me from making the trip up The Hill when she calls." He rolled his head sideways to stare at her with clouded eyes. "I love her, Ellie."

Ellie nodded, suddenly feeling drained. She knew how he felt. She had no right to give Luke advice. Because she was just as foolish. She felt the same way about Jesse. But she hated to see Luke hurt. She and Luke had been friends for eleven years, ever since... But she wouldn't think of that. It was stupid to dwell on the past when there was so much in the present to concern her.

She knew that Palmer still loved Kathleen. Occasionally when his mistress in the next county was busy, Palmer would visit Ellie just to talk. And although he belittled his wife constantly, made fun of her even, Ellie could see the hurt and the desperate jealousy in his face.

The whole thing was crazy, she thought wearily. They all seemed to be caught up in a painful contest from which no one would emerge the winner.

Jesse lay on the wide bed, staring at the shadow-mottled ceiling. Every time he closed his eyes he saw Luke and Ellie. He had never known he had such a vivid imagination. As though he were in the room with them he saw Luke holding Ellie, kissing her, touching her.

Rolling over restlessly, he cursed the fact that he had given up cigarettes. That was one vice he could have used right then.

He sat up sharply when he heard a knock on the door of the motel room. After slipping quickly into his pants, he crossed the room.

Jesse almost laughed when he saw Kathleen standing on the covered walkway. A lavender silk scarf covered her blond hair and she wore dark glasses. Ye gods, he thought, mentally rolling his eyes. A visit from the Texas version of Blanche DuBois was all he needed.

"What do you want, Kathleen?" he asked, too tired to make an attempt at politeness.

She brushed past him, leaving a trail of expensive perfume in her wake. She pulled off the scarf and dark glasses and threw them on the bed, then turned to face him.

Shrugging in resignation, he closed the door and leaned against it.

"I *had* to see you, Jesse," she said, her voice suitably intense.

He raised one brow. "I can't think why...unless you've thought of something else about the night your father-in-law was attacked?"

"No, no," she said, and for a moment her voice held irritation. Then it softened again as she explained. "I'm sorry Palmer interrupted us."

He stared at her for a moment, trying to make sense of her statement. Then he remembered. Kathleen had been trying to seduce him when Palmer had walked in on them.

He smiled grimly. "Kathleen, I'm always glad to see old friends, but I really don't think you should have come here. You're a married woman."

"My marriage was a mistake," she said tragically. Moving across the room, she stopped beside him and clasped his arm against her ample, soft bosom. "It should have been you, Jesse," she said, her voice deep and husky. "But it's not too late for us." She cut her eyes toward the bed. "We can still find happiness together."

"If you're unhappy with Palmer, why don't you get a divorce?" he asked reasonably.

This was obviously not the reaction Kathleen had expected. She frowned, causing the lower part of her face to sag unattractively. Glancing up at him, she sighed heavily. "You don't understand. It's . . . it's a difficult situation. My father doesn't approve of divorce."

He shrugged. "You're a grown woman. You can't let your father run your life."

"But he and Palmer control all the money," she said, as though any reasonable person could have seen that for himself. "So you see, as much as I despise deceit, we'll have to meet clandestinely. I've been thinking about it all evening," she said, her voice eager. "I've worked out a beautiful plan. We can—"

"Kathleen," he said, unwilling to listen to more. "I won't have an affair with you."

She glanced up sharply. "But darling, it's the only way we can be together. I think you're wonderfully noble for resisting temptation, and respecting the sanctity of marriage and all, but—"

"I'm not noble," he said flatly. "I do respect marriage, but that's only part of why I said there would be no affair." He inhaled, his eyes detached as he studied her. "The fairy tales you build for yourself are your own business, Kathleen. But now you're trying to draw me into them, and that makes it my business. This afternoon I tried to show you that

what we had together eleven years ago is dead.
There's nothing left. But you refused to let me tell
you subtly... kindly. You leave me no choice." He
paused. "The main reason I won't have an affair
with you is that the two people involved in an affair
sleep together. That's what it's all about. I don't
want to sleep with you, Kathleen," he finished
bluntly.

Jesse leaned back and waited for the explosion.
There were no vases for her to throw so he assumed
the assault would be verbal. But Kathleen didn't
speak. Her face was contorted in anger, and her
breathing sounded labored. After staring at him with
an expression of pure venom as she clenched and
unclenched her hands, she silently moved to the
door, waiting for him to move aside so she could
open it.

When Kathleen walked out, Jesse moved to the
bed. Leaning down he picked up her scarf and
glasses, laying them gingerly on the bedside table. He
sat down heavily. Jesse knew he should feel sorry for
Kathleen, but he couldn't summon up one ounce of
sympathy. The air in the room was still heavy with
her perfume and it stifled him.

As he lay back he thought of what a vivid contrast Kathleen made to the woman he had been with
earlier in the evening. The blonde didn't come out
well in the comparison.

But then no one would when pitted against his Ellie, Jesse thought. *His Ellie.* That sounded good. He
wished desperately he had the right to call her that.

Eleven years ago he had had the right. But things change.

Closing his eyes, he resigned himself to the vivid, frustrating dreams he knew would come the minute he closed his eyes.

Chapter Thirteen

Jesse drove south out of Bitter. He had no particular destination in mind, but Ellie wasn't home from work yet, and he didn't feel like sitting in his motel room.

During the day he had spent several hours with Sid, catching up on some of the years. Janet, Sid's wife, had welcomed him graciously, treating him like family. Sid had found himself a beautiful woman. And the kids, Jesse thought, smiling. The kids were terrific. It was no wonder that Jesse had left them feeling a little envious of Sid's family.

As much as he had enjoyed himself, Jesse was disappointed that he hadn't had an opportunity to talk to Sid in private. There were so many questions about Ellie buzzing around in his head. He had had to resign himself to waiting for the answers. So now he simply drove and thought, unconscious of the passing miles.

About fifteen miles after the entrance to Dowe Acres, on the same highway, Jesse saw a nightclub. It was built of corrugated aluminum and stood isolated in an otherwise empty field surrounded by a sea of asphalt. It was called The Golden Palace, but, as he drove past it, Jesse decided it didn't look like any palace he'd ever seen.

Suddenly he made a U-turn and went back, pulling the Lincoln into the parking lot. It was freakishly hot for November and he told himself he could use a cool drink. What he really needed was a diversion.

He walked into the club and, taking a seat at the bar, ordered a glass of orange juice from the tall, thin man behind the counter. When it arrived he found it a little tinny, but it was cold, and he drank it gratefully,as he glanced around the cool, dark room.

There were several other late afternoon patrons in the club. A man and woman sat in one of the dimly lit booths, while two older men leaned over a pool table in the far corner of the room. The back of the place was too dark for Jesse to see. The usual pieces of Texan bric-a-brac were displayed on the walls— antique barbed wire, spurs and pistols. Over the bar hung the mounted headgear of a Texas longhorn.

It was the same as a thousand other Texas joints, maybe a little cleaner. The surprise was that it existed at all. Eleven years ago Jesse's father had had to go clear to the next county to get his whiskey.

He felt someone approach to sit beside him and glanced around, frowning when he saw it was Luke Owens. Jesse nodded in an abrupt acknowledgment of the other man's presence, then turned back to his drink. The antagonism from the past was still with them, more strongly on Jesse's side because he was afraid Ellie was having an affair with Luke.

First Palmer, then Luke, Jesse thought grimly. God help him, he had even wondered about Sid until he had met his wife. What was wrong with him?

"You look like you've prospered," Luke said.

Jesse glanced up then shrugged. "I haven't done too bad. I was lucky."

"Still a teetotaler, I see."

Jesse glanced down at the glass of orange juice. Over the years Jesse had learned the value of a social drink, but his had always been nonalcoholic. He had never offered excuses for his abstinence, and after a while he found that the people he dealt with in business accepted any quirk, any behavior when it was combined with supreme confidence.

He glanced at the beer bottle in Luke's hand. "And I see you're still hitting the bottle," he said quietly.

Luke didn't speak for a moment, then he gave a short laugh. "It still galls you to see me with Ellie, doesn't it? It did eleven years ago, and it does now."

"Eleven years ago you liked to beat around the bush, and you do now," Jesse said dryly.

"I just wanted you to know that Ellie and I are friends," Luke said, his voice low and threatening. "Don't try to come between us."

Jesse swung around on the stool. "Look Luke, I don't like you. I never have. But that's not important." He rested his forearm on the bar and leaned closer, his eyes narrowed, his voice tight. "What is important is the fact that Ellie is being talked about because of you. If she hadn't started hanging around with you eleven years ago, people wouldn't be talking about her now. Why don't you just stay away from her?"

Luke stared at him for a moment in blank astonishment then threw back his head and laughed loudly, drawing the interest of the half dozen other patrons of the bar. He took a long drink of his beer then wiped his mouth on his sleeve.

"You're really something, Jesse," Luke said finally, shaking his head. "You want to know the truth of it? You won't like it, believe me. The truth is it's all your fault, not mine." Swinging around on the stool, he sat with his back to the bar, his elbows resting on the counter. He didn't look at Jesse as he continued. "Ellie started running with me and my friends because she figured maybe we would know something about who was messing with your truck the night old man Catlin got his head bashed in. And she was right."

Jesse's fingers tightened around his glass as his heart pounded painfully in his chest. It was a lie. It had to be a lie.

He couldn't think straight. Never in his wildest dreams had he imagined anything like what Luke was telling him. But suddenly he knew it was the truth. In fact, it sounded just exactly like something Ellie would do.

"Who——" Jesse began hoarsely. "Who came forward to clear me?"

Luke shrugged, avoiding Jesse's hard gaze. "What difference does it make? Just be glad someone did. You'd probably still be in prison if they hadn't."

"*Who?*" he repeated harshly.

Luke glanced down at Jesse's clenched fists. "What the hell," he said finally. "It was me. If you remember, I had a score to settle with you. When I saw your truck in the parking lot, I figured it was as good a time as any to get even. I saw you come out of the building before Catlin was attacked. Ellie convinced me to go to the police and give you an alibi." He smiled. "You might even say you owe me one."

All Jesse's muscles constricted. The room was suddenly suffocatingly hot. He hadn't felt this kind of blinding anger in years. He closed his eyes, unable to speak for several minutes. Then he whispered savagely, "What did you charge her for the truth?"

Luke turned to stare at the long line of bottles behind the bar. "Whatever I charged," he said quietly, "Ellie was glad to pay."

Jesse felt the blood drain from his face. Without another word he stood and walked out.

Carrying her bag under one arm, Ellie followed the maid into Mrs. Catlin's private sitting room. She was used to the trip out to The Hill. At least once a month, Mrs. Catlin demanded that Ellie attend her Pekingese, Lu Tsi, nicknamed Lucy.

Ellie walked briskly into the room. Her poppy-colored pants and matching poppy-and-white Hawaiian print blouse made a vivid splash against the pastel surroundings.

"Well, Lucy," Ellie said as the spoiled dog raised her head from the pink cushion. "What ails you today?"

She bent over the dog then glanced up when Mrs. Catlin walked into the room. The elderly woman used her cane, ostensibly to help her get around, but for a long time Ellie had had a sneaking suspicion that she didn't really need it. It was simply that the cane was good for shaking at people who displeased her.

"She's acting very strange," Mrs. Catlin said. "When she gets up to walk around, she only goes a few steps then she stops and sits down. Then she'll get up and do the same thing all over again. It's very disconcerting."

Ellie nodded then picked up the pudgy dog. "Well, let's take a look at you."

A few minutes later she turned back to the older woman. "I'm afraid it's the same old thing, Mrs. Catlin. Your Lucy is simply overweight. I've told you before that she can't handle this many pounds on her small frame. Have you started her on that new diet I gave you?"

When Mrs. Catlin gave her a haughty look, Ellie sighed, knowing the diet had been ignored.

"Mrs. Catlin," she said, trying to hide her frustration. "Lucy will never be healthy until we get some of this weight off her."

"But she hated that diet," the older woman said pettishly. "Couldn't you work up one that she will like?"

Placing Lucy back on the cushion, Ellie looked sternly at the fractious woman beside her. "What you really want me to do is figure out a way that she can eat tons of imported chocolates and raspberry mousse. And I'll tell you again, that stuff is not good for her."

"Oh pooh," she said gruffly. "What do you know about it? Those things don't hurt me. Why should they hurt Lucy? It seems to me that you've been getting awful uppity lately, young lady. You used to have more respect." She glared at Ellie's tight slacks, the deep V of her blouse, and the hair curling riotously around her face. "Can't you do something with the color of your hair? And why do you wear such outrageous clothes? You're supposed to be a healer—a doctor of sorts. Is that any way to dress?"

Ellie hid her smile. Her expression was totally blank when she said, "I have to dress like this, Mrs. Catlin."

The old lady stared at her suspiciously. "Why?"

Ellie leaned closer. "Because the neighbors won't let me put out a red light."

Esther Catlin's gasp of outrage was almost comical. "Scandalous!" she choked out. "You should be ashamed of yourself."

Ellie laughed in genuine amusement. "Oh, I am," she assured her as she walked to the door. "I'll drop by to see Lucy next week." She glanced over her shoulder and gave the old lady a stern look. "See that she sticks to her diet."

She was still smiling as she crossed the hall. But before Ellie had reached the front door, Kathleen walked into the room. "Well, Ella Mae Cooper," she drawled.

"Well, Kathleen Catlin," Ellie said, her gray eyes dancing.

Kathleen didn't like being laughed at. Her thin red lips tightened in anger. "Just what are you doing here?" she asked tightly.

Ellie shrugged. "What do you think? Lucy has indigestion again."

"That damn dog," the blond woman said irritably. "It's nothing but a nuisance. If I had my way it would be put to sleep."

"Somehow I don't think Palmer's grandmother would like that," Ellie murmured.

Kathleen stiffened at her husband's name, then gave Ellie a calculating look. "Jesse's been over here to see me," she said slowly.

"Yes, I know," Ellie said, reaching again for the door. "He told me."

But her casual attitude apparently displeased Kathleen. She reached out to grab Ellie's arm. "You'd better be careful, Ella Mae. You're getting quite a reputation." She raised her arched brows. "I hear there are men at your house at all hours of the night."

Ellie was silent as she studied Kathleen's angry face. "I wonder which one worries you most. Palmer, Jesse . . . or maybe Luke?"

Heated blood flooded the other woman's face. "I'm incensed as any decent person would be at your immoral behavior."

Ellie opened the door, then paused and glanced over her shoulder. "Kathleen, we're not silly teenagers anymore. We're grown women. Do we have to have this same conversation every time we meet?"

Kathleen stared at her for a tense moment then swung around and walked out of the hall, her silence giving Ellie the answer she had expected.

On the drive home Ellie chided herself for letting Kathleen get to her. They should have worked out their differences years before. But maybe Ellie was partly to blame. Reluctantly she admitted to herself that she still resented the Prom Queen. Because she knew that Kathleen wanted them all. Palmer, Luke . . . and Jesse.

Ellie was still agitated when she walked into the living room of her house. She headed for the bedroom to change then stopped and sighed in irritation when she heard a knock at the front door.

Pulling it open, she found Jesse standing in the glaring light of her front porch. She stared at him in open surprise. His face looked strangely tense, as though some powerful battle were going on within him.

"Hello," she said slowly. "I didn't expect to see you tonight."

Stepping past her, he walked to the other side of the room, his movements stiff with some intense emotion. He seemed almost angry when he swung around to face her. "I saw Luke out at the Golden Palace."

She moved to a chair, still examining his tense features as she sat down. "Is that supposed to be significant?" She watched him pace, then said in exasperation, "For heaven's sake, Jesse, sit down." When he turned and sat on the couch, she said, "Now will you tell me what this is all about?"

When he rubbed an unsteady hand across his brow, Ellie saw it wasn't merely anger that was driving him tonight. There was deep suffering reflected in his eyes.

"What is it, Jesse?" she asked in concern.

"Luke said..." He exhaled roughly. "He said the reason you started running with his crowd—with *him*—was because of me. Because you were trying to find someone to clear me." He dropped his hand and stared at her with a kind of agonized bewilderment. "Is it true?"

Ellie sighed, sinking deeper into the chair. "Why on earth would he bring up something like that? My God, Jesse, that was eleven years ago."

"Is it true?"

"Yes, it's true," she said. Her voice had grown heated to match the intensity of his. "Why does that upset you? I would have done the same thing for Sid."

He leaned his head back wearily. "What did you have to do, Ellie, to make him speak up?"

"Jesse—"

"Tell me!" The words were a painful explosion, and Ellie jumped in startled surprise.

"It was no big deal," she said, waving a hand in frustration. "I know I didn't like Luke back then, but that was before I got to know him." She frowned. "It really wasn't fair to him. I pretended to be his girl to gain his confidence. And when he found out what I was doing, he could have made things unpleasant for me. But he didn't."

"Tell me, Ellie."

She stood up abruptly. "Stop making demands. I've told you all I'm going to tell you. I pretended to be his girl."

Jesse raised his fingers to the bridge of his nose and rested his head against his hands. He felt unutterably weary. On the drive back into town several things had become clear to him. Things he should have seen before. The most important was the fact that he loved Ellie. He wondered if he had always loved her. When he had lain with her on the couch the night before, it was the first time he had held a woman without feeling short-changed in some way.

He glanced up. "Is this the reason there's a wall between us? Because out of loyalty to a friend you sacrificed your reputation, only to have that friend desert you at the first opportunity?"

"Don't be stupid," she said, her voice harsh. "I'm not saying it didn't hurt when you left, but I understood."

She was not being completely honest with him. Jesse could feel it. He knew it in his bones. Ellie was holding something back.

Since he had left Bitter, Jesse had succeeded at everything he had tried. Nothing had been too big a challenge for him. Now, when he faced the most important challenge of his life, he was coming up against a brick wall. With the woman he loved he was virtually impotent.

Ellie stood silently watching him. She had never seen him so deeply affected. Not even when he had been arrested. She couldn't understand what was going on in his mind, but whatever it was it was painful to watch.

She stepped closer. "Jesse," she said hesitantly. He looked up and the depth of emotion in his eyes made her catch her breath. "Oh, Jesse," she moaned, kneeling to wrap her arms around him.

He moved into her body as though he would absorb her into his own, pressing his face urgently into her neck. She felt him tremble in her arms and knew how desperately he needed this from her.

"You did it for *me*," he whispered hoarsely. "I was supposed to take care of you. Dammit, it was my *job*. And I let you down. I can't forgive myself."

"No, no," she murmured, spreading kisses across his troubled face. "Don't talk like that. You didn't let me down." Framing his face with her hands, she stared deep into his dark eyes. "Don't you see," she said urgently. "I wanted to do it. It made me feel like I was helping you, like I was important to you."

He brought his hands up to cover hers then turned his head to kiss each of her palms. "You were always important to me. You were the one solid thing I had to hold on to."

His arms tightened around her, trying to draw her even closer to him, his hands caressing her feverishly.

It seemed right when he stood with her in his arms and carried her to the bedroom. At last Ellie accepted her fate. It had been inevitable from the moment he returned that they would make love.

Their clothes were quickly discarded, their movements feverish as the urgency deepened. They had each waited eleven years for this moment and hadn't the patience to wait another second longer than necessary.

When they lay naked on the bed, Ellie cradled his head against her breasts, reveling in the feel of his lips on her heated flesh. She ran trembling hands over his body, exploring him. His body felt familiar but somehow new. And the beauty of him took her breath away. When he moved over her, she was ready, eager to accept him.

This time there was no pain. And there was no hesitation. She knew what he wanted this time, and what she wanted. It was for this that Ellie had shied away from developing a close relationship with a man in the past eleven years. She had been waiting for Jesse.

The tension between them built furiously as they moved together in the ritual of love, straining together to reach fulfillment. Their overheated bodies were covered with perspiration when the climax of their lovemaking burst upon them, bringing wave upon wave of intense pleasure. Then there was peace.

A long time later, Jesse lay quietly staring at Ellie's face. He was filled with love and contentment and gratitude. He had never experienced anything like it, had never known making love could be so intensely satisfying. He recalled women in his past, beautiful, seductive women who were now only hazy faces in his memory. This was different. The fact that it was Ellie had made it different. For the first time in his life, Jesse felt truly at peace with himself.

Suddenly Jesse felt her stiffen beside him. It was happening again. He could feel it. When he reached out to touch her, she jerked away and got up from the bed.

"Don't Ellie," he said. "Please don't shut me out again." He grabbed her hand, forcing her to sit on the bed beside him. "Don't put up the wall," he continued huskily. "I can't stand it. We've got to talk." When she remained silent, refusing to look at him, he groaned. "For God's sake, Ellie. I love you. I want you to marry me."

Ellie had felt numb and drained of emotion. She thought perhaps she would never feel anything again. But now she pressed her hand against her mouth to hold back hysterical laughter.

He wanted to marry her. Now, after all these years, Jesse finally wanted her.

She shook her head wildly. "This—" she waved her hand toward the bed "—won't happen again,

Jesse," she whispered tightly. "It was a mistake. I felt sorry for you and got carried away."

"Is this what happens every time you feel sorry for a man?" he asked harshly. "Just how many men in this town have your pity?"

Reacting instinctively, she drew back to slap him, but he caught her hand, pressing it to his lips. "I'm sorry," he whispered urgently. "God, I'm sorry. That was inexcusable of me. I just don't know what's going on, and it's frustrating as hell."

He lifted her chin, forcing her to look at him. "Is it because you don't want to leave Bitter?"

She shook her head, trying to avoid his eyes, then reached up to push her hair out of her eyes. "Now that Grannie Jean is gone," she said stiffly, "there's nothing to hold me here. I've been thinking about moving anyway."

"Then what is it?" he demanded hotly. "Dammit, talk to me."

"Can't you accept the fact that I don't love you?" she asked, the words deliberate and hard.

His dark eyes darted over her face, searching frantically for something. Something he couldn't find. When the silence became unbearable, he removed his hands from her shoulders and exhaled harshly.

He moved away from the bed to pick up his clothes, not even looking back when he said, "I guess I'll have to, won't I?"

Chapter Fourteen

Ellie sat at her desk. She hated paperwork. She had always hated it. And lately it had been even more unbearable than usual. No matter what she did, no matter where she went, Ellie couldn't get Jesse off her mind.

It had been four days since she had last seen him, since he shocked her with his proposal. That night was still with her so vividly. She had relived it in her mind dozens of times, and each time was more painful than the last. Over and over she saw him as he had dressed and walked out without another word.

She knew Jesse was still in town; his presence caused a constant buzz of gossip. But he had made no effort to get in touch with her.

Leaning her head back against the vinyl chair, she closed her eyes. *I'm doing the right thing, aren't I, Grannie Jean?* she thought wearily. There was too much to forget—too much pain, too much bitterness. The past would always be there between them.

When she heard a noise, Ellie glanced up to see her youthful assistant in the doorway. "Did you want me, Norma?" she asked quietly.

"It's Mr. Baldwin again," Norma said, making a face. "All his Petey needs is the hair around his eyes clipped, but he insists you do it."

Ellie moved her aching shoulder muscles. "Okay, tell him I'll be there in a minute."

Like so many other retired men, Ed Baldwin had too much time on his hands. His wife had passed away several years earlier, and his children were grown and scattered about the country. All he had now was his Scotch terrier, Petey. It was understandable that he was extra cautious with the dog.

Ellie walked into the room where a thin elderly man held a dog on an examination table. "It's good to see you again, Ed," she said, smiling. "Okay, let's see what we can do with Petey."

The procedure wasn't complicated and took only a few minutes, but Ellie checked Petey over just to make the old man feel better. "He's in great shape," she said, then glanced up and smiled. "How about you? Is your arthritis still bothering you?"

"I'm tolerable, Ella Mae. Just tolerable."

He was a sweet old man, she thought. But since his retirement six years earlier, he seemed to have aged twenty years.

Suddenly her eyes grew pensive. "Didn't you used to work for Mr. Catlin, Ed?"

"For twenty-five years," he said, nodding proudly. "First in the lumberyard, then when I hurt my back, I worked as security guard at his office building."

She nodded slowly. "Then you were there the night Mr. Catlin was attacked."

"Bad business, that," he said, shaking his head. "And them never finding out who done it. I think they made a mistake letting Jesse Perkins go. 'Cause he was there that night, all right."

Turning around, Ellie pretended to straighten a tray of stainless steel instruments. "Was Jesse the only one you let into the building that night?" she asked, her voice casual, almost disinterested.

He chuckled. "No, sir, not by a long shot. Mr. Catlin took care of half his business late at night. He was a devil for work, that man. He always said he could get more done when the switchboard wasn't working."

"Who else came to see him, Ed?"

He rubbed his stubbly chin thoughtfully. "Well, there was Burt Cummins from the variety store—he lived over in Pleasant Mound, you know, and used to drive clear to Bitter every day just to run that store. He was a good man, Burt was. Reliable man. Course he's gone now. I heard tell it was a heart attack that got him . . . or was that Vern—"

"Who else, Ed?" she said, swinging around to interrupt him impatiently, forgetting her casual pose.

"Eh?"

"Who was there that night?"

"Well now, let's see . . . there was Mr. Dowe." He nodded. "Yes, he was there. He came pretty late. He had an office on the same floor. And . . . and Palmer Catlin. I guess that was all."

"Did they all come before Jesse?"

He frowned. "Palmer came around pretty early. The others, I couldn't rightly say. It's been a lot of years, Ella Mae." He sounded as though not remembering worried him. "But I told it all to Tom Sharpe."

"Yes, well don't worry about it," she said, her voice soothing. "I just wondered." When he picked up the dog and walked toward the door she said, "Ed, you're sure you told Tom Sharpe about all the others?"

"Sure I'm sure," he said indignantly. His pride was injured now. "I was the best guard they ever had. I knew my job. It wasn't my fault that Jesse Perkins came in and did in Mr. Catlin. I called up and Mr. Catlin said I should send him up. I was just following orders."

"Ed!" she said, her voice shocked. "No one would ever accuse you of being lax in your job. And if anyone ever did, they're crazy."

He nodded his head awkwardly. Ellie was almost sorry she had started the conversation. It was difficult for her to remember that she and Jesse weren't the only ones caught up in the past. Everyone had things they wanted to forget.

Ed had walked out into the hall, but suddenly he turned back to her. "I did tell the police about the other visitors, Ella Mae," he said, his voice stiff. "But Tom knew as well as I did that none of them people would hurt Mr. Catlin. Mr. Catlin was somebody in this town. He was a power that people respected. No, it had to be Jesse Perkins."

She watched him walk away, then glanced at the wall clock. Five o'clock. It was time for her to leave. She chewed on her lip in indecision. Should she wait for Jesse to get in touch with her or should she go to him? She was sure he would want to know what Ed had told her.

Giving herself no time for second thoughts, she removed her long white coat. Then, grabbing her purse, she walked down the hall toward the waiting room.

She would feel much better when she had talked to him about it, Ellie told herself. And there was always the possibility that Jesse wouldn't call her again. She didn't want to think about why she was trying so hard to convince herself that it was necessary to see him.

When she pulled up in front of the Sands Motel, Ellie simply sat there for a moment, staring out the window at the sky. Then drawing in a deep breath, she got out of the car and entered the office. Ellie thought she recognized the chubby brunette girl behind the desk, but couldn't be sure. But evidently the girl had no trouble identifying Ellie. She stared with avid interest as she told Ellie Jesse's room number.

His room was near the front of the motel on the bottom floor, and Ellie walked the short distance. As she raised her hand to knock softly on the door, she exhaled shakily and glanced down at her feet. She had second thoughts about seeing him but it was too late to do anything about them.

Jesse was scowling when he pulled the door open, but his expression changed when he saw her; it became totally blank. Glancing at him nervously, Ellie realized he must have just come from a shower. He wore only a pair of tight black slacks. His chest and feet were bare, his hair damp. Ellie glanced hastily away from his broad chest, keeping her eyes fixed on his face.

"Come in," he said quietly, stepping aside.

In an unconsciously nervous gesture, she held her purse clutched tightly to her chest as she walked into the room. "I didn't want to disturb you, but—"

"You're not disturbing me." He closed the door and moved to lean against the simulated walnut dresser, his hands resting behind him on the edge.

There was no reason why he should make things easier for her, she knew. But she certainly wished he would. The only thing she could do was tough it out. Brushing her hair back, she said, "Ed Baldwin brought his dog to the clinic today." She glanced up at him. "You remember he was the night watchman at Mr. Catlin's office."

He nodded, but still didn't speak. She felt if he didn't stop watching her with that unceasing, dissecting stare she would scream.

Shifting her weight to the other foot, she said, "He told me that others had gone into the building the night Mr. Catlin was attacked. Mr. Dowe was one of them."

He stood up straighter, his brow creasing in concentration. The second he moved, she felt the tension lessen and almost sighed in relief.

"Did Ed say who else was there that night?" he asked thoughtfully.

"Palmer was there before you . . . and Burt Cummins from the hardware store came some time after him. But Ed can't remember if Mr. Dowe and Burt came before or after you."

He nodded. "Then I guess I'd better go talk to Dowe," he said quietly.

Ellie wasn't sure what she had expected to happen next. She had thought maybe they would discuss what Ed had told her in detail. Or perhaps, since the ice was broken, reminisce about their childhood adventures. But whatever she had expected, she was wrong.

Crossing his arms, he ran his gaze intimately over her body. His eyes lingered on the cleavage exposed by her turquoise silk blouse, then drifted down the length of her legs. With lightning speed the tension returned.

Ellie had told him what she had come to tell him, she thought frantically. She should go now. She really should. But like a light-blinded doe, she could only stand there and return his stare.

"Is that the only reason you came?"

The sound of his voice caused her to jump in startled reaction. She had been so deeply involved in their silent duel that the question was almost an intrusion.

Moistening her lips nervously, she whispered, "I just thought you would want to know."

For a moment he stared at her in silence, then slowly he began to walk toward her. "You could have picked up the phone and called me," he said, his voice soft and husky and sensual. "It would have been a lot easier."

She could find nothing adequate to explain her motives. They were every bit as difficult for her to understand. So she didn't speak at all but watched him with wide-eyed, uneasy fascination.

He reached out and slid his hand beneath her hair, letting it rest against her neck, finding the rapid pulse. "Why did you come, Ellie?" he asked.

Suddenly she knew the answer. She had lied to him and to herself. She hadn't come there to give him the information she had gotten from Ed. She had sought him out because she couldn't stay away any longer. That was why the paperwork was unbearable and why she'd slept so restlessly at night, disturbed by vivid, erotic dreams. Because she wanted Jesse so desperately. She caught her breath, feeling her heart pound in anticipation.

"Was it for this?" he whispered, lowering his lips to hers.

Making an incoherent sound of pleasure, she moved into his embrace. Her hands automatically began touching him, caressing him. Leaning her head back, she allowed him access to the sensitive flesh of her throat. His mouth and tongue burned a trail down the length of her neck. His hand moved up to cup her breast, lifting it so that more of the rounded flesh was exposed to his lips.

And when Jesse moved her to the bed, unbuttoning the silk blouse as they walked, she knew the dream that had been plaguing her sleep would soon become reality. And for both of them, it couldn't be too soon.

It was much later when Jesse looked down at her where she lay in the crook of his arm, his gaze drifting lovingly across her face. "This time you're not going to freeze me out," he said softly. "This time there are no barriers."

It wasn't a question. It was a loving statement. He knew she had torn down the wall at last.

She moved her head to kiss his bare shoulder. "I tried that," she said, her voice husky with emotion. "It doesn't work. Even when you're not with me, your memory works to tear down every barrier I try to build." She ran her fingers across his hair-roughened chest. "You always were a bully."

He chuckled softly. Then, staring down to where his dark hand lay on her bare stomach, the fingers spread out across her flesh, he said, "Stay with me tonight."

Ellie wanted so badly to tell him yes. The thought of spending the whole uninterrupted night with Jesse made her shiver. But it wasn't possible. Not tonight; perhaps not ever. She needed time to think.

"I can't," she said, her regret showing on her face. "I promised Sid and Janet I would have dinner with them. In fact, I have to go now or I'll be late."

For a moment he looked as though he would argue, then he smiled wryly. "I'm jealous of Sid and Janet. I'm even jealous of the kids."

When he leaned down to kiss her, Ellie clasped his neck with both hands, holding him tightly to her. "Oh, Jesse," she whispered urgently. "I'm so confused."

He had known that even before she spoke. It was written on her face. But he couldn't understand the cause. There were so many things he didn't understand about Ellie. When they had made love she couldn't have been more loving, more open. Why couldn't she open her mind to him as well? If only he could get her to talk to him, he thought. He couldn't fight this invisible enemy without her help.

But at least now he had hope. She had come to him. She wanted him. That was something, he told himself. He would give her time. Everything began with the first step.

"Don't worry so much," he said gently. "We'll work it out. Whatever it is, we'll work it out."

When a shadow crossed her lovely face, Jesse felt a deep fear invade him. He wanted to pull her back to him and keep her there forever. Nothing could be allowed to come between them. Not now, when they had finally found each other.

Feeling helpless, he lay on the bed and watched her dress. She held on to the bedside table while she slid into her shoes. Then suddenly she went strangely still and the silence began to draw out. When she slowly turned around, he saw she was holding Kathleen's scarf between forefinger and thumb.

"She certainly is a busy lady," Ellie said dryly.

Jesse kept his eyes on her face, watching her carefully. "She came here to make me an offer," he said flatly. "I refused."

Raising her gaze, she searched his face. Apparently she found what she was looking for because suddenly she grinned. "I didn't see any cuts or bruises on you. What did you do—hide the vases?"

He chuckled, loving her more than ever. "Will you let me see you tomorrow?" he asked hopefully.

For a moment she looked doubtful, and his muscles tightened in anticipation of her refusal. Then she exhaled and smiled brilliantly as she nodded her agreement, leaving him with the memory of her beautiful face.

For a while Jesse simply lay where he was with his hands behind his head. He felt empty without her. He supposed he should get up and have dinner, but he wasn't hungry. On the other hand he was too keyed up to stay in his room. Shifting restlessly, he decided he might as well go and see Dowe.

Kenneth Dowe had apparently picked up his ex-partner's habit of working late because when Jesse called his house Jesse was told he was still at the office.

Minutes later when Jesse stepped from the Lincoln and approached Dowe's office building, it seemed that he was living a rerun. The building was new, but on another night eleven years earlier he had gone to see another of the most powerful men of Bitter.

After clearing Jesse's visit with Mr. Dowe, the guard allowed Jesse to go up, as another guard had in the past. Stepping off the elevator, he walked down the long carpeted hall. Before he reached the suite, the door swung open.

"Jesse," Kenneth Dowe said, his voice jovial. "It's good to see you. Come in, come in."

As Dowe ushered him into the outer office, Jesse glanced around at the elaborate suite of rooms. He hadn't seen Kathleen's father since the older man had visited Jesse in jail eleven years earlier. It hadn't been a pleasant visit.

Now, Jesse could tell Dowe was in a quandary. He still saw Jesse as a no-account kid from the wrong part of town. But on the other hand Dowe couldn't afford to offend him. He knew that Jesse could bring money to his town and his businesses. He also knew that Jesse could buy him ten times over. A sharp businessman like Dowe would have looked into Jesse's finances the minute he hit town.

"Well, Jesse," he said as he settled in his chair behind the huge leather-topped desk. "Things have changed for us all, haven't they? I hear you're looking for a building site for a new plant. I'm sure you can find something here to suit you. If you need any help with the local officials, you just give me a call. I'll take care of it."

Jesse smiled. "I'll keep that in mind. Actually I didn't come here to talk business."

"Oh?" The older man frowned. "What can I do for you?"

"I thought as long as I was in town I would try to find out what happened to John Catlin eleven years ago," Jesse said, his voice expressionless. "I know the official opinion was that he was killed by a transient, but I wanted to sort everything out for myself."

Dowe frowned. "I can see how you would be interested," he said. "But I don't know how I can help you. I think their final decision was the only one they could have reached. To be frank, when your innocence was proven there were no other suspects."

"What about you?" Jesse asked carefully.

"What are you talking about?"

It hadn't taken much to make Dowe lose the affable pose. His eyes revealed deep anger, looking very much, in fact, like Kathleen's, Jesse thought.

"I heard that you were in Catlin's building that night yourself," Jesse said.

"What does that prove?" he asked tightly. "My office was there and we frequently held meetings at night."

Jesse glanced around the office then back to his host. "I also heard you benefited by his death."

"That's vile!" he exclaimed, his voice harsh. "Who told you that?"

"It doesn't matter," Jesse said. "Did you see Catlin that night?"

"I was with him about a half an hour before you were." He was now actively hostile, and the words sounded as though they were forced out of his mouth. "And I can tell you right now that if you drag up that old tragedy and try to connect my name to it, you'll find a slander suit waiting for you."

"What you tell me won't go beyond this office. I'm not trying to get revenge. I'm merely curious." He paused. "If you saw him before me then the only one who could have been there after me was Burt Cummins."

"No, Burt was there at the same time I was. Palmer was the only one he was expecting to come late."

Jesse sat up straighter. "Palmer? I thought he was there early."

A strange look crossed the older man's face. He obviously regretted having spoken. "Yes, that's right," he said hastily. "He was there early in the evening."

Jesse inhaled slowly. "You're hiding something. If I have to I'll go to the police and I'll go to the mayor...and I'll go to Kathleen. But one way or the other, I'll find out."

The threat was an effective one. Dowe had stiffened at the sound of Kathleen's name and now looked resigned.

"All right," he said sharply, his eyes full of resentment at having his hand forced. "When Palmer came to see his uncle early in the evening, John didn't have time to talk to him. He told him to come back about midnight...but if you think Palmer had anything to do with his uncle's death, you're crazy. What's more I think you've got a lot of nerve to come back after all this time and start stirring things up."

Jesse didn't listen to half of the older man's tirade. His mind was stuck on what he had told him about Palmer. Had Palmer gone to see his uncle after their confrontation at the Pixie? If so why hadn't Ed seen him?

"Do you know why Catlin wanted to see Palmer?"

He hesitated, then stood up. "Yes, I know," he said stiffly. "And it's none of your business."

Leaning forward, Jesse said stiffly, "Look, I have no intention of trying to get the police to reopen the case. I simply want the facts. After what happened to me, don't you think I'm entitled to know?"

Jesse stared at the man's stiff back, knowing the silence was his answer. As far as Kenneth Dowe was concerned, Jesse had no rights.

Jesse's fingers dug into the arms of the chair. He hadn't wanted to bring Kathleen into this, but he would do what he had to do to get answers.

"Did you know that Kathleen is the reason I'm here in Bitter? She thought she had solved the mystery so she wrote me several letters." Jesse hesitated; he owed nothing to Kathleen. "She thought you had hired someone to assault Mr. Catlin and then set me up."

As Jesse watched his back, Dowe seemed to shrink. His shoulders sagged and the tailored suit didn't fit him quite the same.

When he turned back to Jesse, he had gained control once again, his expression blank. He walked back to the desk and sat down in the leather chair, and when he spoke again, it was as though he were resuming a polite conversation.

"I probably should have said something at the time...but I didn't and there's no use regretting it now. John was having trouble with Palmer. When he told me about it he was angrier than I'd ever seen him. Palmer had been writing checks and signing his uncle's name to them. John said he would straighten Palmer out once and for all." He glanced down at his desk. "I've never mentioned this to anyone. Not even to Palmer. I'm not trying to make excuses for myself. I did what I thought was right at the time. I had complete faith in Palmer's innocence. I still do. Telling the police what I knew would have served no purpose."

Jesse understood. He didn't think it was right or ethical, but he understood. Kenneth Dowe had wanted Palmer for a son-in-law. It was a good move, a prudent move. He wasn't the kind of man to make things hard on himself.

Jesse stood up. "I guess that takes care of why I came," he said wryly.

"What are you going to do now?"

"You did what you thought was right," Jesse said, his voice dry. "That's exactly what I'm going to do. I'm going to talk to Palmer and find out what happened."

Chapter Fifteen

The next morning Jesse made the trip to The Hill for what he sincerely hoped was the last time. He was sick to death of the past. But he wanted to get it out of the way so he could concentrate on his future—his future with Ellie.

Sooner or later she had to tell him what was bothering her. Together they would make it right. For the rest of his life, he wanted nothing more than to make things right for her.

When Palmer's office had informed him that Mr. Catlin was working at home that day, Jesse had almost decided to forget the whole thing. He wasn't sure if the truth was worth another confrontation with Kathleen. That was one strange lady, he thought wryly. And if there was any way to avoid her on this visit, he would.

But it was Kathleen herself who opened the front door for him. "Jesse!" she said, her voice filled with surprise and delight. "What a wonderful surprise."

One brow shot up in astonishment. Jesse had expected cold hostility at the very least. He should have known Kathleen would manage to reconcile his behavior with her fantasies.

"I just knew you would change your mind, darling," she said eagerly. "Come in, please."

She moved aside for him to enter then glanced toward the back of the house and frowned. "I wish you had called first. I could have met you somewhere." She leaned closer to whisper, "Palmer's home today."

"Actually that's why I came out," Jesse said. "I'd like to see him."

She looked puzzled and a little insulted. "Well of course, if you've got business to take care of. But promise you won't leave until we've had a chance to talk."

He smiled but made no reply, wondering if there was a side door he could use.

Leading the way down the hall, she opened the door to Palmer's study. "Palmer, Jesse's here to see you."

Palmer leaned back in the high-backed leather chair and watched Jesse walk into the room. "Wonderful, I need a treat today," he said dryly. "Come in, Jesse. Sit down."

Kathleen stood by the door, her hands clasped before her, her reluctance to leave obvious as she gazed at the two men. Jesse hid his smile. She was probably afraid Jesse would tell Palmer about her midnight visit to his motel room.

Palmer stared at his wife for a moment, then shrugged and glanced back at Jesse. "What can I do for you?"

"I just need some information, Palmer," Jesse said. "I went to see Mr. Dowe last night."

"How brave of you," Palmer muttered.

Jesse studied the other man closely. "I wanted to talk to him about the night your uncle died."

For a moment Palmer stared in silence, then he glanced down at his desk, avoiding Jesse's eyes. "Oh yes? Well I guess it's only right. You've stirred up the past for a lot of people just by being here. I don't see why my dear father-in-law should be spared." He hesitated, playing with a gold pen on his desk. "And what did you find out?"

"I found out that if what he told me is true, Dowe couldn't possibly have been the one who killed your uncle."

Palmer's head jerked up in astonishment, then he started to laugh heartily. "You mean you actually accused him of that? God, I would have given a fortune to see his face." He inhaled unsteadily. "So, what else did he tell you?"

Jesse suddenly found his role a little distasteful. Palmer was obviously worried. Jesse wasn't going to punish him by dragging out the suspense. "Mr.

Dowe told me that your uncle was expecting to see you that night."

"Everyone knows that," Palmer said, waving his hand casually. "I went to see him early in the evening."

"No, I mean he expected to see you later," Jesse said quietly. "Around midnight."

Jesse had forgotten that Kathleen was still in the room. But now she moved forward to stand beside Jesse's chair. "What are you saying, Jesse?" she asked. She tried to smile, but she was obviously puzzled as she glanced swiftly from Jesse to her husband then back again.

"I'm saying that Palmer could have been there after I was," Jesse said quietly.

"Jesse," she said in a husky scold as she laid her hand on his sleeve. "You're kidding, aren't you? Look, you don't have to do this." She glanced at her husband out of the corners of her eyes then back to Jesse, making the gesture significant. "Jesse, I think I've made it obvious how I feel. You don't have to drag out all this just to get at Palmer. *It's not necessary*," she said with tight emphasis.

He exhaled in exasperation. "Kathleen, this has nothing to do with you. This is between Palmer and me."

There was more than confusion in her eyes now. Fear widened her pupils. She backed away from Jesse, her gaze searching frantically for her husband. "You're trying to accuse Palmer of killing his uncle," she whispered in harsh disbelief. "You're crazy! You won't get away with this," she said urgently. "Do you hear?"

"That's enough, Kathleen," Palmer said calmly.

She moved behind the desk and stood next to her husband, her hand on his shoulder. "But it's incredible. He can't come back to town and start making these wild statements."

Palmer laid his hand over hers and squeezed it. "Don't start worrying, Kathy," he said, his voice soothing. "You know how high-strung you are. You have to take care of yourself. Nothing's going to happen to me."

Jesse watched them silently. And suddenly he realized something that shocked him. As unbelievable as it seemed, these two people loved each other. It was a strange kind of relationship, he thought, but then who was he to judge?

"Go on, Jesse," Palmer said. "What else did my father-in-law tell you?"

Jesse shifted in his chair. Suddenly he had had enough of the past. He had wanted to find the truth. But what difference would it make to his life? Absolutely none that he could see. Did he have the right to satisfy his curiosity at the expense of these two people?

"I think I've changed my mind, Palmer," Jesse said. "This doesn't really matter anymore. It was eleven years ago. Kathleen's right. There's no need to stir it all up now."

Palmer leaned his head back as though he were suddenly weary. "He told you about the checks, didn't he?"

Jesse nodded.

"That's what I thought," he said, smiling grimly. "You didn't know my uncle, Jesse. I tried to tell you what he was like that night at the Pixie." He shook his head. "He could make you feel like you were nothing, less than nothing. He had these spiteful little tricks he enjoyed playing on me. He would lead the conversation in a certain direction, goad me into making a statement, then make me feel ridiculous by showing me how stupid the statement was. By the time I was in college, we hated each other." He stared over Jesse's head as though he were getting a glimpse of hell. "We really hated each other," he whispered tightly.

"Palmer," Kathleen said nervously, bending over him, grasping his arm tightly. "Darling, what are you saying? You don't mean it." She rounded savagely on Jesse. "You see what you've done?" she hissed. "What right do you have to come in here and make him say these things? You should never have come back."

Kathleen certainly had a convenient memory, Jesse thought ruefully. She had forgotten that she was the one who had sent the letters that had started the whole thing. In effect, she had sent for him.

Palmer pulled her back around to face him, staring into her eyes. "It's time, Kathy," he said softly. "It's time it was all out in the open."

Closing her eyes, Kathleen shook her head violently. "No, it's not. I don't want to know. You don't have to say anything. Make—make Jesse leave, and then we can go back to the way it was. We can just forget this happened." She dropped down to kneel beside him. "Please, Palmer."

He stared at her for a moment then slowly shook his head. "I can't. You see it's not for him, it's for me."

Tears formed in her eyes. "But it hurts you, Palmer," she whispered.

He pulled her into his lap, cradling her head against his shoulder, then raised his eyes to Jesse. "After you left the Pixie that night, I followed you. I figured I would wait until you left then keep my appointment with Uncle John." He smiled cynically. "I was hoping he would be so angry with you, he would forget about the checks I'd written."

As he spoke, he absentmindedly stroked his wife's hair. "I hung around in the parking lot, getting more nervous by the minute. When I saw Luke fooling around with your truck, I moved into the shadows so he wouldn't see me. I didn't feel like having a run-in with him. And anyway I would have enjoyed seeing him trash your truck," he added, smiling. "When you left, it was by a side door, which was why Ed didn't see you leave. I remember you stood in the doorway for a second, then saw Luke at your truck. When you started running, I caught the door before it closed completely and went up to Uncle John's office."

He sighed. "He was mad all right. But his anger at you only made what he felt for me worse. He started in on me again. He threatened to have me arrested for the checks. I couldn't take it anymore. I couldn't just sit there and let him run me down. I told him to go ahead. It would hurt his reputation as much as it did mine." He shook his head. "I've never seen him so furious. Before, he was always coldly, deliberately angry. That night he lost his head completely." He closed his eyes, as though the memory were too much. "You remember that cane he always carried? He didn't need it, but somehow it made him feel powerful. Grandmother uses it now, and it makes me sick every time I see it."

He exhaled slowly. "He picked up the cane, and I swear he was going to beat me with it. I was scared, Jesse. I just wanted to get out of there. I—I got up to leave, but he was too close. So I dived at him." His fingers tightened on Kathleen's hair. "I caught him off guard and he went down, hitting his head on the corner of the desk. I saw blood running down the side of his face, and my mind just went blank. I couldn't think what to do. I kept imagining what he would do to me when he woke up. So I ran."

Kathleen was weeping noisily in Palmer's arms, her hand on his neck in what could have been a protective gesture.

Jesse didn't know what to say. He couldn't believe Palmer had been carrying this around for all these years. It must have been pure hell.

"I never intended for you to be blamed," Palmer continued, his voice tired. "I try to tell myself that if it had come to a trial, I would have gone to the authorities." His smile was self-mocking. "I try to tell myself that, but I don't know if I believe it." He exhaled roughly. "So. What comes next? I suppose you'll go to the police with this."

Jesse had no intention of going to the police. It was an accident pure and simple. If Palmer could live with the knowledge that he had inadvertently been the cause of his uncle's death, then Jesse wasn't going to change that.

But Jesse didn't get the chance to tell him so. Kathleen jumped up, her eyes wild as she stared at Jesse. "You can't," she said desperately. "It was all a mistake. You can see that. Palmer didn't know that his uncle was badly injured. He made a mistake, for God's sake. Everyone makes mistakes." Her laugh was a desperate sob, her eyes panicked. "Your precious Ellie, for example. She—she made a mistake, too."

"No, Kathy," Palmer said sharply.

"Why not?" she asked, never taking her eyes off Jesse. "Why shouldn't he knew that when you start digging in the past some unpleasant facts are bound to come to light? Let's see how he feels when he hears about a mistake someone he loves made *eleven* years ago."

Her eyes glazed with fear, her face contorted with anger as she continued. "When Ellie was running around with Luke and his crowd, the habit of smoking and drinking wasn't all she picked up. She also picked up a *baby*, Jesse." She smiled viciously. "Your precious Ellie got herself pregnant. Everyone in town knew all about it. And her miscarriage didn't change the fact that she had gotten pregnant. There's no one here that will let her forget what she is. She's a *whore*," she spat out. "A cheap, no-good whore."

Jesse moved forward. He didn't know if he would have struck her, but he didn't get the chance. Palmer slapped her first, then he caught her in his arms and began to rock back and forth, comforting her as she sobbed against his shoulder.

"Palmer," she said jerkily, her voice that of an injured child. "Why... why did he do it? Jesse's supposed to be wonderful. But he hurt you." She pounded her fist against his shoulder. "And... and he wouldn't sleep with me." Her voice rose to a wail. "He wouldn't make love to me, Palmer."

"Hush, darling," Palmer soothed, wiping her eyes with his handkerchief. "Don't cry so. You'll make yourself sick. It doesn't matter. He has no taste, no discrimination. Anyone would want to make love to you... anyone."

As he watched the strange scene between Palmer and Kathleen, Jesse stood perfectly still, but a muscle twitched at the corner of his grimly set mouth. Then slowly, his movements stiff like those of a weary, old man, he turned and walked out of the room.

Chapter Sixteen

Jesse drove away from The Hill, his face drained of color, his knuckles white as he held the steering wheel in a death grip. The scenery along the highway went past unseen as the drama with Kathleen played itself over and over again in his head.

She got herself pregnant. While you were in jail, she got a baby.

He couldn't get beyond that. He couldn't use logic to work it out. He just kept hearing the words, as the blood pounding in his ears kept time. Without realizing what he was doing, he drove straight to the clinic.

The waiting room was empty when he walked in. Without pausing, he went straight to the receptionist.

"I want to see Ellie," he said, barely able to get the words out of his constricted throat.

The blond girl behind the glass window stared at him strangely, as though something about him made her nervous. "I'm sorry, sir. She's out on a call. Could her assistant help you with something?"

He shook his head, feeling his nerves tighten painfully. "When will she be back?"

"She won't be back today at all." She hesitated, staring at his clenched fists. "Is there something I can do? Are—are you ill?"

In frustrated silence, he turned and walked out. As he approached his car, he saw Sid's station wagon pull into the parking lot and turned immediately to walk toward it.

"Hey, Jesse," he said, smiling. "I was just coming to see if Ellie wanted to take in a movie with us tonight. Why don't—" He broke off abruptly, staring at Jesse with narrowed eyes. "What's wrong?"

Jesse grabbed Sid's arm, unaware of how his fingers dug in. "Sid, Kathleen said that while I was in jail Ellie got pregnant," he said bluntly. "Is it true?"

Sid inhaled sharply, then shook his head. "I'm sorry, Jesse," he said quietly. "That was a stupid thing for her to tell you."

"Is it true?" Jesse repeated harshly.

Sid leaned against the station wagon and glanced around the parking lot as though he were suddenly uncomfortable. "Hell, Jesse, I left town right after you did. All I can tell you is what I've heard."

"Then tell me."

"It wasn't long after I got back that I started hearing rumors. Actually Janet heard them first and asked me about it. She likes Ellie and was concerned."

"What kind of rumors?" Jesse asked tightly.

"That she had gotten herself pregnant, then had miscarried when she was about two months along." He grimaced as though he found it distasteful to repeat the rumors. "You know how gossip is, Jesse. I've heard enough of it to last me a lifetime. Ellie never mentioned it herself. I figured if it was true, it was painful for her so I never brought it up. But I knew that was the reason everyone talked about her and watched everything she did. You know this place, once you get a reputation, it's impossible to get rid of." He smiled wryly. "Ellie's way of fighting it was to give them more to gossip about."

All through Sid's explanation Jesse had kept a tight hold on his emotions. If he didn't he was afraid he would start screaming. He hadn't really needed the confirmation from Sid. Deep down, he had known at once that it was true. And this was the key to the way Ellie had been acting. Someone had hurt her badly. It was no wonder she was afraid to give her trust to Jesse.

He glanced at Sid. "Everyone keeps saying she got herself pregnant," he said tightly. "But she didn't do it by herself. Did the gossips happen to say who the father was?"

Sid shook his head, his eyes sympathetic. Jesse realized then that he must have shown more of his feelings for Ellie than he knew.

Inhaling deeply, Jesse turned away, his fists clenched tightly as he walked toward his car.

"What are you going to do?" Sid called after him.

"I don't know," he ground out. "Maybe I'll find Luke and beat the living hell out of him."

He slammed the car door just as Sid yelled, "No, Jesse, wait! You're wrong about Luke."

But Jesse had had enough of talking. He felt like beating his fists against a wall. Someone had hurt Ellie. And someone had to pay.

Ellie gathered up the papers that were on the seat beside her, then stepped from the car. She had been sitting all day with a sick cow, and she was bone tired. As she fitted her key into the lock, she heard a car pull up in front of the house.

Turning around, she saw Jesse get out of the silver Lincoln. She smiled, lifting her hand to wave. Then, as he walked closer, the smile froze on her face and Ellie stepped backward, feeling an emotion very close to fear. Something had happened. She saw it in his pale face and in the stiff, awkward way he moved.

She inhaled shakily, unable to speak when he reached her. Opening the door, she walked inside, leaving him to follow.

He moved a few steps inside the room, then swung around to face her. "Why didn't you tell me?" The words sounded harsh, as though it were painful to speak. "Why did you let me find out through gossip?"

Oh, God, she thought frantically. He knew. Jesse knew. She stared at him silently, her thoughts feverish, her face pale.

When she didn't answer, Jesse raked his fingers through his hair, pacing in agitation across the living room. "Did you think I would feel guilty when I found out? Guilty for getting into trouble so that you had to try to fix it. Guilty because when you needed me most, I deserted you." He slammed his fist into the back of a chair. "Well, you're damn right. I feel guilty. I feel guilty as hell. If I hadn't been in jail, Luke would never have gotten his hands on you. By God, he wouldn't have gotten you pregnant." A muscle twitched near his lip. "But he'll pay," he whispered hoarsely. "As soon as I can find him, he'll pay."

The laughter that escaped her was a harsh, ugly sound that grated on the ear. Jesse's head jerked up to stare at her in surprise. This obviously wasn't the reaction he had expected.

"The baby wasn't Luke's," she whispered savagely, her voice unsteady with the intensity of her emotions. "It was yours, Jesse. It was *yours.*"

He looked as though she had slapped him, but she couldn't stop now, not once she had already started. She had held it in too long already.

"That night in the cabin. You finally decided that was a dream, didn't you? It wasn't a dream, Jesse." She could see the truth dawn in his eyes. "And it wasn't Kathleen. It was poor, dumb Ella Mae Cooper." She laughed again, pressing her hand to her lips. "You were so drunk, you didn't know what was happening. But I didn't realize that. I thought you knew. When you touched me, when you held me, all I could think was 'Jesse wants me at last.'"

She rubbed the back of her hand across her eyes and was surprised to find her face wet with tears. "After we made love, I thought...I thought it meant that you loved me, too. I thought that we would be together forever like I had always dreamed." She paused, drawing in a raspy breath. "Then...then you said Kathleen's name. And I knew that you didn't even know it was me." She put two fingers to her lips and rocked forward a little, trying to stop a moan from forming. "Too bad it wasn't Kathleen that got the baby," she whispered painfully.

His face was drained of all color and for a moment she thought he was going to pass out. There were beads of perspiration on his brow, and his dark eyes looked frantic as though there were things going on inside his head that he couldn't keep up with. When he moved at last, it was to draw a trembling hand across his eyes. He opened his mouth to speak, but no words came out.

Slowly, stiffly, he turned and moved toward the front door. He didn't say a word as he left but shut the door quietly behind him.

Ellie sat down heavily in a chair. Time passed unacknowledged as she sat there unmoving, unthinking, unfeeling. Eventually she stood, picked up her purse and walked outside to her car.

She drove the sports car as close to Otis Bates's hill as she could, then she got out and walked. Ellie hadn't climbed the hill to the cabin in eleven years.

The path was overgrown and the brambles tore at her stockings.

The sun was low on the horizon when she reached the cabin. It was nothing more than a standing pile of wood now. A good wind would blow it away. She stared at it for a moment then glanced away.

Moving slowly she walked the short distance to the swimming hole. Here it was the same. Time hadn't corroded the trees or the cool clear water. Lowering herself to a large boulder, she sat and silently stared into the pool.

The air had gone soft and gray with dusk, and the frogs had begun to sing when she heard the footsteps behind her. She didn't turn. She knew who it was immediately. She should have known he would find her.

Jesse sat on a low rock a few feet away from her. Picking up a pebble, he chucked it into the water. For a moment the frogs fell silent, then when they began again they sounded almost angry at the intrusion.

"Otis should tear down the cabin," he said softly. "Someone could get hurt in it."

Someone did get hurt in it, she thought dully, then said, "Yes, everyone has told him before that it's a hazard. He said he would take care of it, but you know how slowly things move around here."

He smiled slightly, nodding. "I'll never forget the time Otis caught us skinny dipping. I was fourteen and you were only nine. Lord, I thought he was going to have a fit." Ellie could feel his eyes on her as he talked. "I've never run so fast in my life. It's a good thing nobody saw us both running off the hill, carrying our clothes, both naked as jaybirds. I bet it took me an hour to get all the stickers out of your feet."

He fell silent and when Ellie glanced at him out of the corner of her eye, he was staring down at his hands. Suddenly he looked up and caught her eyes. "Why didn't you tell me, Ellie?" he asked gently. "Not this time, but eleven years ago. Why didn't you tell me?"

"When was I supposed to tell you?" she asked quietly. "Should I have told you when you were in jail, going out of your mind with being cooped up, not knowing if you were going to prison for a crime you didn't commit? Or should I have told you the night you came to me to tell me you were leaving? You were all fired up with the thought of making a new and better life for yourself. Is that when I should have told you?"

For a tense moment there was only the sound of the frogs. Then he exhaled and said, "No. You couldn't have told me. I'm not blaming you. I'm just finding it a little hard to believe."

"You don't believe you were the father?" she asked, staring straight ahead.

He said something vicious under his breath. "That's not what I mean and you know it. As soon as you told me, it all fell into place. Of course it was you that night. It couldn't have been anyone else. I should have known all along... I wish I had."

She heard the deep regret in his voice and it moved her against her will. Slowly she began to speak.

"When you left I thought the pain would never stop. But it did. I started thinking about the baby instead. Even the awful, awful look of disappointment on Grannie Jean's face when I told her didn't stop me from being glad about the baby. I was counting on that baby, Jesse. I wanted it desperately." She made a small sound in the back of her throat, a sound of pain. "You put that baby in me. It was a part of you. And I wanted it. God, how I wanted it. But then, about two weeks after you left—"

She broke off as a shudder shook her body. "Grannie Jean said that the miscarriage was God's will...but she wanted the baby, too, Jesse." She brushed a hand across her eyes. "She was so strong. And I shamed her in this town, but she still wanted her grandchild. She cried when I lost it. I had never seen Grannie Jean cry, but I was glad someone could cry for my baby. Because I couldn't. After that the gossip got real bad. Grannie Jean never lost her dignity, but I knew she heard the gossip. She fought it even in her own friends. She and Grampa, they helped me survive that time."

Shifting positions, she let out a long breath. "After that I felt lost. I didn't have you. I didn't have the baby. I thought I would die from the hurting." Ellie could see Jesse's hands shaking, but she couldn't stop talking. She had to tell it all. "It got better after a while. But I couldn't forget you. Sometimes a whole day would go by when I wouldn't think of you, then something would happen. I would see a place or hear a song and your face would come back stronger than ever. Sometimes I thought I hated you. I just wanted your memory to leave me alone so I could get on with my life.''

Jesse sat there as though he had been turned to stone. Her words were killing him. He felt every minute of her pain and humiliation as though he had lived it himself. No wonder she found it so hard to be around him. He must bring it all back for her when she wanted so badly to forget.

He wanted to hold her, to comfort her. But Jesse was afraid, more desperately afraid than he had ever been in his life.

Standing, he walked to the edge of the pond. Without looking at her, he began to speak.

''I told you I came back because I needed a plant site and because of those letters. I wasn't being entirely honest. Those things were only incidental. There were two very real reasons why I came back.'' He turned to face her. ''The first was the look on your face when I left that night. After all those years I still couldn't get it out of my mind. I thought someone here would be able to tell me what happened to you, where you were.'' He paused, inhaling unsteadily. ''The other reason was what happened that night in the cabin. Maybe I didn't know it was you, but I did know that nothing else in my life measured up to that. Every relationship that I tried to build with a woman was nothing compared to what I had felt that night.''

He stared at her face, praying his words would get through to her. ''Ellie, I would give my life to have spared you the pain that you went through because of me. You've got to believe that. Over the years when I thought of Bitter I was always surprised to find a kind of yearning in my thoughts. I always thought that it was because I wanted to show people here that I was finally somebody. But that wasn't it. It was because you were here, Ellie. All my memories of you were here."

He waited, praying that she would understand. That his words, his feelings would make a difference. But she didn't move. And Jesse died a little inside.

He had failed. He would always remind her of the pain. Slowly, awkwardly, he began to walk away. Slowing his steps and without turning around, he said softly, "I love you, Ellie. And as much as I want to, I can't change the past. I would if I could. I would make it all go away for you. All I can do is try my damnedest not to screw up the future."

He stared down at the ground, his nerves stretching to the breaking point as he waited for her reaction. But there was none. Keeping his head down, he began to walk.

He had taken only two steps when she began to speak, her voice barely audible over the night sounds.

"You know the worst part?" she whispered. "It was when I realized that after all that had happened, after all I had been through—and had put Grannie Jean and Grampa through—after all that, I realized that I still loved you. I felt so spineless when I discovered that nothing would ever change the way I felt about you." Her breathless laugh was almost a moan. "All I ever wanted in my whole life was to be Jesse's girl," she said with painful intensity.

Emotion raced through him in a painful streak. He wanted to grab her and hold her and never let her go. But he was still afraid of making any sudden moves. Turning, he walked cautiously toward where she sat. "The past is gone, Ellie. We can't bring it back and relive it. We've got to think of the future. And all I can offer you for the future is the role of Jesse's woman...Jesse's wife...Jesse's love. If you want it— please, Ellie, please want it—they're all yours."

He heard a sob catch in her throat, then she stood and walked into his arms. And he knew this time it was forever.

Chapter Seventeen

Esther Catlin stepped from her car and waited for her chauffeur to help her friend Regina out of the back seat. A cold snap had swept through the night before and her breath frosted the air. The temperature was unusually low, even for December. Wrapping her mink more closely around her, she glanced around sharply when she heard a horn honk several times, raucously disturbing the peace.

"Who was that?" Regina asked, staring as two people waved from a bright red sports car.

"That was Ella Mae Cooper and Jesse Perkins," she said, her voice stiff with disapproval. "I heard that she was leaving town with him. All I can say is good riddance to bad rubbish."

"But Esther," Regina said. "Who'll take care of Lucy? What will happen to your poor little dog?"

Suddenly Mrs. Catlin raised her cane to shake it after the car. "Ella Mae Cooper!" she shouted. "You come back here, girl! You hear me?"